Breaker

Breaker

Annemarie Allan

Kelpies

Kelpies is an imprint of Floris Books

First published in 2009 by Floris Books
© 2009 Annemarie Allan

The publisher acknowledges a Lottery grant
from the Scottish Arts Council towards the
publication of this series.

British Library CIP Data available

ISBN 978-086315-682-3

Printed in Poland

This one is for Max in a Million
and for Sarah, environmental hero

Chapter 1

"Take Toby down to the beach. He can have a nice long run there. And when you get back, everything will be warm and cosy. That's a promise!"

The front door closed. Tom frowned as he tugged on the lead, pulling Toby out of the path of a passing car. "If Mum was so desperate to get a dog," he grumbled, "why isn't she the one who's taking him out for a walk?"

"She can't," said Beth. "Dad's gone to the dump with a pile of rubbish and the plumber's coming to fix the central heating."

"Well, at least it's a break from lugging boxes up all those stairs," said Tom. "After yesterday and this morning, my arms feel like cooked spaghetti."

Tom lurched forward as Toby jerked on the lead, almost choking himself in his hurry to move on. Beth zipped up her jacket and cast a doubtful glance up at the sky, where a line of dark grey cloud was swiftly eradicating the small patch of blue.

Toby didn't care about the fat drops of rain splashing on to the pavement. Stumpy tail wagging furiously, he scurried along the narrow street and dashed across the road towards the stone steps leading down to the beach. A stream of people passed them, heading for shelter. Already, the wide expanse of sand was deserted except for one solitary family gathering children and packing up their belongings. Umbrellas were popping up everywhere.

Toby looked up, waiting for Tom to unclip the lead. The children stood shivering in the cold wind blowing in off the sea.

"What about the Centre?" Tom gestured to the Sea Bird Centre perched on the headland like a giant wooden sailboat washed up on the rocks. "We could look at the Bass Rock on the webcam. Find out what the birds are up to."

"I don't need a webcam. I know what the birds are up to," said Beth. "They're standing around in the rain, just like me." She squinted through the steadily increasing drizzle at the looming bulk of the rock thrusting up out of the water. "Why is it so white?"

"Work it out," said Tom. "There're a lot of birds out there."

Beth looked at him. "You mean they live on a mountain of poo?"

"Yup." Tom grinned.

"Yuck." Beth looked back at the water. A host of little sailing boats were heading for the harbour. Out beyond the rock she could see a massive ship outlined against the darkening horizon. It didn't seem to be moving at all, though it was hard to tell at that distance.

A zigzag flash of summer lightning split the sky, followed a moment later by the deep rumble of thunder. Beth turned away. A ship that size probably didn't need to worry about the weather.

Toby whined in disappointment as they left the

beach and made their way up the path to the Sea Bird Centre. Tom stopped at the big glass doors and peered inside, wondering if he could trust Toby to behave. From the look of the crowd milling about inside, it seemed that most of the refugees from the beach had headed for the nearest available shelter.

Tom pointed to a sign just above their heads, declaring that "assistance" dogs were welcome. "Doesn't that mean ordinary dogs aren't allowed?"

"Maybe we could pretend he's a guide dog," suggested Beth.

Tom looked down at Toby. "No chance." Toby looked up at him and wagged his tail. Short and scruffy, with a black patch over one eye and a bad habit of wandering off in whatever direction smelled most interesting, there was no way they could expect anyone to believe Toby was a highly trained guide dog.

Beth didn't bother to argue. She knew he was right. "What about the museum then?" she said.

"Closed," said Tom gloomily. "A bit of the roof fell off."

They turned away and wandered aimlessly back across the road. Beth slowed down to gaze longingly through the steamed up windows of a café. The door opened and she took a deep breath, relishing the delicious aroma of fish and chips.

"I think we should go home," she said. "It's raining. Mum wouldn't want us to stay out if it's raining. We could go upstairs, out of the way and do some more unpacking."

Tom thought for a minute, but then he shook his head. "I don't think so Beth. It's really cold up there. The windows don't fit properly. And if Toby doesn't get his walk now, then we'll probably just have to take him out later."

"Just because you're twenty minutes older than me doesn't give you the right to order me about," grumbled Beth, but she perked up at the sight of a small white van drawing up outside their new house. It looked as though the plumber had arrived.

"There's always the Tourist Information Office," said Tom.

"But we're not tourists. Not any more," said Beth. "We live here now." Beth always liked to get the facts straight. Usually just before she bent them.

Tom was losing patience. "It's better than nothing, isn't it?"

"Okay," said Beth agreeably, thinking that maybe by the time they got back, the heating would be on and their damp and chilly new house might be a bit more comfortable. "At least we'll be indoors."

Bedraggled, they made their way to the Tourist Office and squeezed inside. A voice on the radio was droning its way through a weather report that nobody needed to hear. It looked like everyone who hadn't made it into the Sea Bird Centre had come here instead.

There was even another dog, a tiny thing with a jewelled collar and a tartan bow on top of its head. Its owner took one look at Toby and scooped the little dog up into her arms.

Toby shook himself, sending splatters every-where. The woman behind the desk tutted and went off to fetch a mop while Tom and Beth headed for a display stand in the corner out of the way of everyone else.

"Look Tom!" Beth pulled out a leaflet. "That's our new house!"

The picture on the leaflet showed a huddle of narrow, three-storey fishermen's houses, all painted in different colours. At the far end of the street, sea and sky blended together in two differ-ent shades of blue.

Tom studied the picture, wondering why it looked familiar. Then he had it. "It looks just like Balamory."

"Well it's not Balamory," snapped Beth. "It's North Berwick." She reached out and laid her finger on the little window right at the top of the house. "That's supposed to be my room," she said. "Instead I'm camping on your bedroom floor."

"I haven't got a bed yet either," Tom pointed out.

"No," agreed Beth, "but at least your room doesn't have a broken window and wallpaper hanging off the walls."

She opened up the leaflet and stared down at a picture of the Sea Bird Centre. Behind it was North Berwick harbour, nestling in the shelter of the headland. With a snort of disgust she jammed the pamphlet back in the stand.

The woman with the mop had finished wiping the floor and was back behind the counter, but she was still looking at them. Uncomfortably conscious of her eyes boring into the back of his head, Tom crossed the room to the information board. Beth stood behind him, her breath hot on his neck as he scanned the adverts for holiday activities and places to stay.

"What's that?" he said at last, pointing to a bright green card right in the middle of the board.

"It's YOUR river." Beth read aloud. "Help keep it safe. Join People Opposing Pollution … that's POP!" She grinned at Tom and carried on reading. "Open meeting in the Jubilee Hall, Sunday 14th June."

"That's today," said Tom. "And look!" He pointed to a small pink post-it stuck to the bottom of the notice. "It says 'dogs welcome!' What do you think of that, Toby?"

Toby didn't seem in the least bit interested. He had found a leaflet of his own and was busy tearing it to shreds.

"Can I help you with anything?"

They whirled round to see the mop lady standing right behind them. She bent down and snatched up Toby's well-chewed leaflet. Ignoring his whine of disappointment, she said: "Was there something in particular you were looking for?"

"We've found it, thanks," said Beth. "Come on, Tom. Let's go."

She headed for the door, too busy concentrating on making a dignified exit to notice the sudden silence. As the door swung shut behind them, every head in the room turned towards the voice on the radio.

Chapter 2

Jubilee Hall was on the High Street, a huge Victorian building with tall windows and round, gothic turrets on the roof. Tom hesitated outside.

"This looks kind of posh," he said.

"It also looks nice and dry," said Beth. "Let's get inside."

Together, they climbed the wide stone steps and found another green notice stuck to the massive front door.

"POP inside and join today," read Beth.

"POP ... that must be People Opposing Pollution," said Tom.

Another pink post-it was stuck to the bottom. It was soggy from the rain and the ink had run, but it was still more or less possible to read. Beth's eyes lit up. "It definitely says dogs welcome."

The heavy wooden door opened with a gothic creak, revealing a huge, dimly-lit entrance hall. Directly ahead of them an elegant staircase led up into the gloom. The walls were hung with dark portraits of men with huge beards and old-fashioned clothes, who looked down in deep disapproval as Tom and Beth's damp shoes squeaked across the polished wood floor. They stopped and looked around.

"There's nobody here," said Beth.

"Clever of you to notice," said Tom.

Somebody sneezed and they both jumped.

"Who was that?" whispered Beth.

"No dogs in the building," said in a hoarse voice.

Beth looked up in disbelief at the nearest portrait, then tried to pretend she hadn't when a man emerged from the darkness behind the staircase.

"Sorry kids," he said. "Guide dogs only."

Tom's face fell. "Not again."

The front door creaked open and they turned to see a small, grey-haired woman in a red bobble hat walking towards them. She smiled pleasantly.

"Afternoon, Mike," she said. "POP?"

Beth stifled a giggle. She didn't dare look at Tom, knowing that he, too, was struggling not to laugh.

"Just down there," said Mike, his eyes fixed on the woman's dripping umbrella. "Third door on the left."

Deeply envious, the two children watched her march confidently across the hall and down the corridor. The sound of a door opening was followed by a clamour of voices. One, louder than the rest, was yelling for everyone to shut up and listen.

"Sounds exciting," said Beth.

Mike pulled out a hankie, blew his nose hard and then moved forward, herding them towards the front door. "Come on kids, out you go."

"But the sign says dogs are welcome." Beth said stubbornly.

"And it's raining," added Tom, as if that might somehow make a difference.

"I know it's raining," growled Mike in a hoarse, cold-sodden voice. "Muddy puddles everywhere. I'm not even supposed to open on a Sunday, you know."

Beth was determined to have one last try. "It definitely says dogs welcome."

He scratched his head. "Are you sure?"

Beth nodded firmly. With a defeated sigh, he gave his nose another wipe and followed her to the front door. Tom trailed along behind with Toby. Beth hauled the door open and pointed to the note.

Frowning, Mike stared down at the post-it. "Is that an arrow?" He reached out and traced one of the smudges with his finger. "Ah," he said, his frown clearing. "You want the professor. Angus likes animals. He thinks they should have the same rights as humans. Come on. I'll show you."

The children followed him down the steps and back into the street.

"Go along there, then down the alley past the rubbish bins. There's a set of steps leading to the basement." He grinned at Tom's doubtful frown. "Don't worry, son. Everybody knows Angus. He's a professor at Waverley University. Daft as a brush, but perfectly harmless. He's even done one or two school visits."

"But what does he ...?"

Tom never got to finish. There was a scuffling noise from behind the front door, followed by a manic giggle. Mike wheeled round and hurried back inside, leaving Tom and Beth standing in the rain.

Mike's voice was exasperated. "How many times do I have to tell you? You know you're not allowed down here on your own! Where's your brother?" This was followed by a volley of sneezing that stopped abruptly as the heavy door swung shut.

The children exchanged a puzzled glance, then Tom jerked forward as Toby tugged at the lead. They followed him along the wet pavement until they arrived at a narrow alley lined with wheelie bins.

"Did you see that woman in the hat?" Beth stopped and looked back resentfully. "I bet they're all just like her … ancient and boring." She gave her brother a thoughtful look. "But there was definitely something going on in there. Maybe you could look after Toby for a minute while I nip back in and take a peek."

"Why me? Why don't you look after him?"

They glared at each other, dangerously close to a quarrel, before Beth gave an apologetic shrug.

"Sorry," she said. "It was worth a try."

"I suppose it was," said Tom. He would have suggested it himself if he'd thought of it in time. He looked down the alley, trying to see past the wheelie bins. "I'm not sure about this."

"You worry too much, " said Beth as she set off down the alley. "It's got to be better than getting soaked."

By the time Tom caught up with her, she was halfway down a flight of rusty iron steps. Toby jerked the lead again, pulling Tom headlong down the slippery steps, across a puddle and through the open door at the bottom.

He found Beth standing beside a rickety little table, flicking through a large notebook "It's a visitor's book," she said, putting it back on the table. "But it doesn't look as if anybody's signed it."

They peered into the gloomy interior. All they

could see were a few pieces of discarded furniture and some lumpy objects covered in dust sheets.

"There's nobody here," Beth observed.

Tom tilted his head, listening intently.

"What's that noise?"

Beth concentrated. After a moment, she heard a glooping, burbling sound coming from a dim corner right at the back.

"This is spooky," Tom said. "Let's go!"

He turned back, but it was too late. A tubby figure came bouncing down the steps towards them. In spite of the weather, he was dressed in a short-sleeved shirt and a pair of baggy corduroy shorts. A wild brush of snow-white hair peeped out from beneath a dripping tweed cap.

He stopped at the foot of the stairs and gave them a beaming smile. "I'm so sorry I wasn't here to welcome you when you arrived." He bowed deeply. "Allow me to introduce myself. My name is Professor Angus MacBlain."

Beth whispered in Tom's ear. "He looks like Father Christmas on his holidays."

The professor's smile widened. He didn't seem to notice that he was standing in the puddle. "And you are?"

Tom kept a firm grip on the lead. He didn't think the professor would appreciate being jumped on by a wet and dirty Toby. "I'm Tom," he said. "And this is my sister, Beth."

The professor nodded. "I'm very pleased to meet you, Tom and Beth." He bent down and held out a hand to Toby, who leaned forward and sniffed at it eagerly. "And who is this?"

"That's Toby," said Tom.

"Glad you could make it, Toby," said the professor. He smiled up at the children. "I have to admit, I was a little worried that no one would come. It's a little out of the way down here. I presume you're here for the demonstration?"

The children nodded, a little uncertainly.

"Excellent!" said the professor, as Toby wagged his tail and licked at his outstretched hand. "It's always so heartening to see young people take an interest. I think you'll find it lots of fun ... and very educational too."

Beth frowned, slightly suspicious of what this odd little man meant by educational. "We came for the POP meeting upstairs. About the oil tankers," she said, hoping the professor wouldn't ask any awkward questions. She didn't know very much about oil, or tankers, or pollution. "But they wouldn't let us in because of the dog."

"I was a founding member of POP, you know." The professor's face drooped. "But now they won't let me in either. Even though I know more about this stretch of coastline than anybody else. There have been ... issues." He glanced uneasily at the open door behind him.

"Issues?" Beth asked.

The professor didn't seem to hear. He turned back to the children and his face brightened. "I'm sure you won't regret taking the time to stop by. Mike told me I could set up down here. Not terribly easy to find, I admit, but plenty of room. He's a friendly chap, Mike."

"Doesn't like dogs much," muttered Tom as his

eyes swept doubtfully round the dingy basement.

There didn't seem to be anything wrong with Professor MacBlain's hearing this time. "Ah well," he said breezily. "I don't suppose he can do much about the rules." He waved an arm. "This way please ... there's a lot to see."

Tom slid a questioning look towards his sister. Beth shrugged.

The bubbling noise grew louder as they followed the professor across the room towards a lumpy object shrouded in a large white sheet. With a theatrical flourish, Professor MacBlain whipped off the sheet to reveal a large fish tank standing on a metal trolley.

Beth and Tom stared at the cables snaking out from both sides of the tank and the complicated-looking knobs and dials on the front. Inside, there was nothing except clear water and a large pile of shells lying on a heap of sand.

"What are we looking at?" asked Tom.

"*Mytilus Edulus,* of course," said the professor. "That's mussels to you. Hmm ... Let's see ..." He tapped one of the dials. "Ambient light seems fine. I just need to regulate the salt content and adjust the water temperature ... okay ..."

Reaching down the side of the tank he produced a flat metal plate and slid it down against the back wall of the tank. "Right. Now let's create some movement to stimulate adhesion." Seeing the blank look on the children's faces, he added, "I'm just going to stir it." He pulled a pen from his shirt pocket and dipped it into the water.

Tom and Beth leaned closer, watching the mussels move, slowly at first, then faster and faster, until the whole tank was a swirling vortex of madly spinning shells.

The professor whipped the pen away and there was a tremendous thump as every single mussel walloped against the metal plate at the back of the tank. Toby let loose a surprised bark and the children jumped back in alarm as the tank lurched backwards and forwards from the impact.

The professor's hands shot out to catch it just before it toppled to the floor. "Feisty little beggars, aren't they?"

He settled the tank back on to the trolley, gazing at it with the air of a proud father. "They'll do this anywhere, given the right conditions."

Beth leaned over to whisper in Tom's ear. "You know, I think this might be fun after all!"

Chapter 3

Frowning, Tom pulled Toby away from the water that had slopped on to the floor. Somehow, Beth's idea of fun always seemed to end up with trouble for both of them. "Isn't it a bit dodgy?"

"Oh come on, Tom." Beth elbowed him in the ribs. "Where's your sense of adventure?"

Tom scowled. Beth smiled sweetly at him then turned to the professor.

"I never knew mussels could do that."

"Well, they don't normally react quite like this," admitted the professor, "I've been setting up my own mussel lines. These ones are specially bred to produce more glue than usual. They seem particularly fond of metal, but they'll stick to just about anything."

"What's it for?" asked Tom.

The professor waved an enthusiastic arm. "The potential applications are enormous! An environmentally-friendly glue, totally organic and extremely powerful. I contacted the Post Office, but it seems that stamp collectors don't like it if they can't get the stamps off the envelopes." He shifted the tank a little further from the edge of the trolley. "This is really just a spin-off from my main project."

"What's your main project?" Tom asked.

Once again, the professor didn't seem to hear. "Let's leave them in peace for now, shall we?"

Carefully, he spread the sheet back over the top.

"I thought it was great," said Beth. "Very dramatic."

"This way, please." The professor led them across the room to an old-fashioned wooden wardrobe leaning up against the wall. He bent down and looked Toby in the eye.

"Toby," said Professor MacBlain, "I think what I have here will interest you in particular."

Toby wagged his tail.

"This bit is really just for fun." The professor tapped the wardrobe. "The important bit is over there."

He reached with one foot and nudged the plastic tube that snaked out of a hole in the side of the wardrobe and across the floor, before it disappeared inside a clear plastic box about the size of a shoebox.

"My eco-friendly fuel cell," the professor bent down and tapped the box. "Easily transportable … energy where and when you need it. And all components biodegradable, of course."

The box contained a set of dull grey cubes, balanced one on top of the other. Beth frowned. None of this looked very impressive.

Tom was staring at the wardrobe door. "Beth," he said slowly. "Can you see anything … odd?"

Beth tilted her head and stared at the door. She blinked. Was there a thin line of light around the edge?

"Well done, Tom!" said the professor. "I see you've noticed. This isn't just any old wardrobe!" He bounced forward and pulled open the door.

Both children gasped in amazement. The inside of the wardrobe was awash with colour; a patchwork of sparkling greens and browns that shone with a soft clear light.

"Bioluminescent moss," said the professor. "No need for an external light source. The moss does it all for you!"

"But what is it?" Tom was mystified. It might look nice, but that didn't turn it into anything but a brightly-lit wardrobe.

"An indoor pet walker of course." The professor waved at the green and brown walls. "A nice woodland walk. Even when it's raining outside. Look!"

The children looked. The bottom of the wardrobe was missing.

"Conveyor belt down here," the professor went on. "You can take a walk, get some exercise and at the same time you can help save energy!"

"How?" Tom didn't see how the dog walker saved energy. "Don't you have to use energy to get it to work?"

The professor winked. "Wait and see, Tom. Wait and see. All I need now is a volunteer." He raised his eyebrows and looked at them expectantly.

Beth had scrunched up her eyes to make everything blurry. When she did that, the scene inside did look a little bit like a path through the woods.

Tom couldn't resist. He gave his sister a firm push forward. "Come on, Beth. Where's your sense of adventure?"

She shot him a look over her shoulder. Tom smiled innocently.

"Wonderful!" The professor rubbed his hands.

"If you'd like to step inside? And Toby as well, of course."

Tom handed Beth the lead. She climbed inside the wardrobe, reaching out with her free hand to touch the moss that covered the inside of the wardrobe door.

"It's really soft," she said. "And warm." She laughed and pulled Toby inside. "Narnia here I come."

The professor closed the door. "Right," he said. "If you'd just like to start walking?"

Tom heard a rumble from inside the wardrobe as the conveyor belt began to move. "Are you okay, Beth?"

"Fine." Her voice was muffled, but she sounded perfectly calm. "It's nice in here. All sparkly."

"Watch the fuel cell, Tom," said the professor.

Tom saw first one, then another of the blocks begin to glow with a soft, yellow light. "I get it!" he said. "You're using the conveyor belt to power it up!"

"Well done," said the professor. "The energy from the conveyor belt is transferred to the cell." He raised his voice and called out to Beth. "Could you perhaps move a little faster ... run maybe?"

The footsteps inside the wardrobe turned into heavy thumps. Beth was doing her best to follow Professor MacBlain's instructions.

"Excellent," said the professor. "The cell is almost fully charged. I think we can afford to add in a gentle breeze." He reached over and pressed a switch. Tom heard the sound of a fan starting up and then Beth's voice from inside.

"Magic!"

All the little blocks in the fuel cell were glowing now. It was like a miniature sun, lighting up the dingy basement with bright yellow light.

The thumping stopped abruptly and Tom's attention snapped back to Beth. There was a whine from Toby and then his sister's voice, worried now.

"Oh no ..."

Tom rushed forward and began pulling frantically on the door handle. "Get her out of there!"

"Don't worry." Professor MacBlain joined him. "The door's just a little sticky ... ah ... here we go!"

The door swung open and Beth appeared. She was staring at Toby. All his fur was pointing the wrong way, but he didn't seem frightened. In fact, he looked quite pleased with himself. He jumped across a small puddle and out of the wardrobe. Beth followed, red-faced with embarrassment.

Tom stared at the puddle. "Sorry," he said at last. "Toby's a rescue dog. From the animal shelter. We only got him last week and he's not properly house-trained yet."

"Not to worry." The professor peered at the puddle. "Obviously something I failed to take into account. Not your fault either, Toby," he added.

Tom glanced at his watch and was surprised to discover that they had been out for nearly an hour.

"We'd better go," he said.

"But I have so much more to show you!" The professor waved in the direction of various other shrouded objects.

Sorry," said Tom. "We've got to get back."

The professor's face fell. "Perhaps just one more thing?"

"All right," said Tom grudgingly. He knew Beth was just waiting for the opportunity to volunteer him for whatever the professor had in mind. "Just one."

"Excellent!" The professor dived into his pocket and pulled out a small black box. He unfolded it up to reveal a tiny screen and a tiny keyboard. "Palm-top computer," he said. "Very useful when you're on the move." He dug in his pockets once again and held up a thin plastic rectangle. "Flash drive."

Tom and Beth stared at him blankly.

"You probably call it a memory stick," he said. "It's got a very interesting piece of software. I'm teaching the computer to talk."

"That's nothing new," said Beth. "I had a talking computer when I was small."

Tom shook his head. "It didn't really talk, Beth. It just had a set of things it trotted out when you pressed the right button."

"That's right," said the professor. "A computer can learn millions of words, but it's the way words fit together that they have trouble with. The grammar." He stuck the memory stick in the side of the computer and pressed some keys.

"Grammar!" Beth was disgusted. Did he really expect her and Tom to enjoy a computer lesson in grammar? "That's pants!"

"Explain pants."

The children looked at the professor in surprise.

It was his voice, but the words were coming from the little machine in his hand.

Professor MacBlain nodded encouragingly. "Go ahead," he said. "It's programmed to pick up on anything it doesn't understand."

"It means something's rubbish," said Beth, a little self-consciously. It felt odd to be talking to a machine.

There was a long pause. *"Explain pants."*

Beth had the impression that if the machine had fingers, it would be drumming them by now. "I just did!" she said.

"It knows the word," said the professor. "It just doesn't understand what you meant when you used it."

"Pants are something you wear," Beth was beginning to regret getting into this. "Under your trousers. But it means something's rubbish as well."

"Trousers," said the computer. The words came out slowly, almost thoughtfully. *"A cloth covering for the legs and lower body."* After a very long pause, it spoke again. *"Your pants are rubbish."*

Beth's mouth dropped open. Tom laughed She stared at the little machine, in surprise.

"I'm teaching it to make jokes," Professor MacBlain chuckled quietly. "You'd be surprised at how many serious-minded people are trying to explain jokes to computers."

"What for?" Beth demanded.

"Well," said the professor. "It teaches them not to take everything literally. If I can talk to the machine and it can talk to me, I won't need anybody else's help with my ..." He broke off suddenly.

"Main project?" Tom suggested.

But the professor had gone deaf again. He closed the palm top and removed the memory stick. "I think it's time you went home," he said. "We wouldn't want your parents to worry. But perhaps you might come again?"

"Definitely," said Beth. "I haven't had so much fun in ages!"

They got as far as the stairs before the professor suddenly yelled, "Wait! You haven't signed the visitor's book!"

With a deep sigh, Beth took her foot off the bottom step and turned towards the rickety little table. She hated visitor's books. She could never think of anything clever to write. After some intense thought, she scribbled wildly for a moment, then slammed the book shut and hurried up the steps after her brother.

"I liked the professor," said Tom as they edged past the wheelie bins.

"So did Toby," answered Beth. "Did you notice he was wearing odd socks?"

"Toby?" Tom was only half listening.

"No, stupid," said Beth. "The professor."

"If you ask me," said Tom, "Absolutely everything about the professor was odd." He looked at Beth thoughtfully. "I wonder what his main project is."

"Well, we're going back, aren't we? Maybe we'll find out then." Beth's eyes gleamed. "I can't wait to see what else he's got."

But their cheerful chatter halted abruptly when they reached the end of the alley and saw that the rain-swept street was alive with people, some carrying shopping, others dragging children along behind them, all hurrying past the Jubilee Hall and down towards the harbour.

Chapter 4

More people were surging down the steps of Jubilee Hall, including Mike, the caretaker, and the woman in the red bobble hat. Soon, there was no one left except two men in business suits, one tall, one short, looking just as confused as the children.

"What's happening?" said Beth.

"I don't know," said Tom, "Let's take Toby home and then see what's going on."

The plumber was in the hall banging the radiator with a spanner while Mum hovered nearby, an anxious look on her face. She nodded in a distracted way when they told her something was going on, so they quickly pushed a reluctant Toby into the kitchen and re-emerged from the house to join the crowds still heading for the shore line. In the distance they could hear the wail of emergency sirens growing gradually louder.

By the time they reached the open space around the Sea Bird Centre, it was alive with people, surging this way and that; everyone pushing and elbowing their way towards the front of the crowd. Tom was very glad they hadn't brought Toby along with them.

He stumbled and nearly fell as someone shoved past, almost knocking him to the ground. He opened his mouth in protest and then shut it again as he recognised the plumber, tearing off his work

overalls as he fought his way towards the doors of
the lifeboat station.

"What's going on?" a voice asked. "He got a
phone call and then just dropped everything and
took off."

The children turned to see their Mum standing
just behind them. She had come out without even
a jumper and her bare arms were crinkled with
gooseflesh.

"I don't know," said Beth. "I can't see anything."

"There's more room down there." Tom pointed
to the beach steps.

Mum nodded. "Stay close behind me," she
ordered, as she hurried down the steps and began
to work her way forward. Her gasp of horror when
she reached the shore set Beth frantically wrig-
gling to catch up with her.

"What ...? What is it, Mum?" Beth's eyes followed those of the rest of the crowd as she finally
caught sight of what had drawn so many people
out of their homes on such a miserable day.

The ship she had last seen on the horizon was
now much closer to the shore. It was even larger
than she had imagined, rearing up out of the water
like a floating castle. Tom arrived beside her and
Beth heard his indrawn breath. Together, they
watched the ship roll sideways with every wave as
it headed slowly but inevitably towards the towering bulk of the Bass Rock.

"It's massive," said Tom, his voice an awed
whisper. "That bit at the front is longer than a
football pitch. Two football pitches!"

The man beside them was wringing his hands and swearing softly, over and over.

"Sorry," he said, when he noticed the children. "It's just … a nightmare come true."

"But what's happened?" snapped Mum.

"It was on the radio," he answered. "That tanker was waiting for the tugs to escort it upriver. Lightning hit the bridge and knocked out the steering system. They can't control where they're going and the wind is driving them towards the Bass." He wiped what looked suspiciously like a tear from the corner of his eye. "It she hits the rock," he said hoarsely, "Then God help us all. And God help the folk on board."

"I don't understand," said Beth. "We're not in danger, are we?"

"There're millions of gallons of crude oil on that ship," said a woman standing nearby. "What do you think is going to happen if it holes itself on the rock?"

Hardly daring to breath, the children watched the tanker tilt towards the towering shape of the Bass Rock. A fierce gust of wind splattered rain into their faces and when they looked again, the ship was surging forward.

"She's going to make it," whispered the man. "Come on, come on! Just a little bit further …"

But he was wrong. The tanker suddenly heaved to one side and a moment later, the wind brought the sound of a tearing, rending crash. Everything went still. Not a single person in the crowd was moving. Even the wind had dropped. Then suddenly, everything leaped into life once more. The doors to the lifeboat station burst open. The lifeboat swept down the slipway and landed in the water with a gigantic splash. Helicopters circled the tanker, churning up the waves. People were yelling, turning to each other, talking and gesturing wildly.

"Come on," said Mum, her voice heavy. "There's no point in staying here. We're just in the way. We'll get more information off the radio."

They walked slowly back, past an array of emergency vehicles and an army truck disgorging a row of grim-faced soldiers in camouflage gear. Tom counted three ambulances, two fire engines, about five or six police cars and several green vans with the East Lothian Ranger service logo on the side. Another van with a huge satellite dish on top was making its way down the narrow street.

"That'll be the television people, I suppose," said Mum. "Looks like North Berwick will be making tonight's headlines."

Tom looked back as they opened the front door to see order beginning to emerge from the confusion. People were directing the vehicles, sending them this way and that, while others were busy unloading all kinds of strange equipment that he didn't recognise.

"It's weird," Beth said in his ear. "One minute it's just an ordinary Sunday afternoon and then we're in the middle of all this."

Tom nodded. Beth was right. The everyday world had suddenly spun off into chaos.

Dad arrived home not long afterwards and they spent a miserable afternoon around the radio. After the first breathless report, the news bulletins rehashed the same information over and over. The tanker, *Nora Gallow,* had collided with the Bass Rock. Emergency services had been mobilised and local residents were advised to stay at home and wait for further information.

Two hours later, the plumber staggered back indoors and collapsed into the nearest chair. The family gathered round him, eager for news.

"Are you all right, Brian?" Mum asked, shoving a hot mug of coffee into his eager hands.

He nodded. "Piece of cake," he said. "We're usually out in weather much worse than that."

"What about the crew?" asked Dad.

"The captain requested evacuation. We got them all off safely. They've been taken to the Community Centre. And there's some more good news," he said, "if you can call anything about this good. The tanker's holed all right, but there's been almost no spillage. Looks like the rock has plugged the hole ... for now, at least."

"So what happens now?" asked Beth.

Brian shrugged. "They can't move her. Not without opening the hole in the side. I suppose they'll try to transfer the oil and then see about pulling her off. But that could take a while. The ship's lying at an angle. It'll complicate any ship to ship oil transfer."

He handed back the cup and stood up. "I'd better get my things together and get home," he said. "No more work today, I'm afraid."

Dad wanted to see things for himself so Tom and Beth walked back down to the harbour with him. A steady stream of people was heading in the opposite direction, mostly grim-faced and silent except for a few who were laughing and chattering, their eyes alight with excitement.

"Look at them!" Beth was disgusted. "You'd think it was some kind of free show."

"Some people have no imagination," said Dad. "They have no idea what this might mean."

The film crew were still there, in front of the Sea Bird Centre, with the tanker in the background; a dark, ominous shape half-hidden by the rock. But most of the emergency services were already packing up. Dad stood silent for a long time, staring out across the water.

"Let's go, kids," he said at last. "There's nothing we can do here."

Chapter 5

The tanker dominated the news on every television channel all that night, but by the next morning, the tone of the news bulletins was a little calmer. Divers reported that the tanker had collided with an underwater spur of rock. For the moment, at least, it was not leaking significant amounts of oil.

After yesterday's dramatic events, both children were surprised and disappointed to discover that Mum and Dad expected them to carry on with life almost as normal.

"This is a stupid idea," said Beth as they left the house and headed up the road to their new school. "There's only a week to go before the holidays."

"We thought you might as well get to know some of the locals before the summer starts," said Dad, pressing the entry buzzer. "The way things are now, though, I doubt if you'll be having much fun on the beach." He glanced anxiously at his watch. "I hope this doesn't take too long. I've got a train to catch."

The head teacher introduced herself in a distracted sort of way, then she hurried them down the empty corridors, gabbling all sorts of information too fast to make any sense. She opened a classroom door and led them inside to meet the rest of Primary Six. Tom and Beth followed her lead, uncomfortably aware that every eye in the room had swivelled round towards them.

Grateful that their new teacher did nothing more than make sure that everyone knew their names, Tom and Beth quickly found themselves a couple of vacant chairs, where they were left alone to get used to things.

It was easy to blend into the background. They had arrived in the middle of a discussion about whether tankers should be allowed on the river and it seemed like everyone had something they wanted to say. The argument bounced to and fro, but despite the babble of voices, no one added anything new to what Brian the plumber had told them yesterday.

At lunchtime, they sat in gloomy silence on a bench in the playground. Tom stared longingly at a crowd of boys who were kicking a football around.

"I feel like everyone's watching us and ignoring us at the same time," said Beth.

She shoved the last of her sandwich in her mouth and walked over to the bin, then jumped back in surprise when she spotted a very small and extremely grubby boy hiding in the space between the bin and the wall. At least, she thought it was a boy. It was hard to tell because he was covered in mud. Boy or girl, it was obvious he didn't belong in this part of the playground.

He walked out from behind the bin, wiped his nose on his filthy sleeve and looked up at her. "I saw you."

Beth gave him a friendly smile and bent down to talk to him. "Are you from the nursery?"

The boy didn't smile back. He stared at her

accusingly. "I saw you at my house. My daddy wouldn't let you in."

"But I've never been to your house," said Beth.

"Yes you have. I saw you."

She looked across at Tom. "Do you think we should take him back where he belongs?"

Tom didn't answer. With rising hope, he was watching one of the footballers detach himself from the crowd and head in their direction. Maybe he would get to play after all.

But when he arrived, the other boy simply nodded at Tom and Beth. Then he said, "Right, Jacob. Back you go. You know you're supposed to stay inside the fence. I don't know how you always manage to find your way out."

Jacob grinned. "I dug a hole," he said. Then he frowned ferociously. "I'm not going, Connie. I like it here. With you."

The other boy scowled. "I told you, Jacob. You have to call me Connor. And you can't stay here." He cast a longing glance at the football game. "I have to take you back."

"He says he saw us," said Tom, hoping to start a conversation. "He said your dad wouldn't let us in."

"Must have been at Jubilee Hall," said Connor. "We live in the flat upstairs. Dad's the caretaker. Were you there for the POP meeting?"

"Sort of," said Tom.

"But we ended up down in the basement," said Beth.

Connor raised an eyebrow. "With Professor MacBlain? Did he show you his dog walking machine?"

Tom nodded. "It was very ... interesting." He didn't want to be rude about the professor, but he needn't have worried.

Connor grinned cheerfully. "He's crackers, isn't he? That's why they make him stay in the basement."

"They?"

"POP," said Connor. "People Opposing Pollution. The professor helped set it up, but he's got some strange ideas. There was some kind of argument. Dad wouldn't tell me what it was about."

"So why don't they just get rid of the professor if they don't want him there?" asked Beth.

"It's not as easy as that." Connor laughed. "He's like his superglue. Impossible to detach!"

"I thought he was good fun," said Beth. "And he seems really keen on being green."

"Well, POP's all about protecting the river," said Connor. His eyes drifted back to the football game. "There's a demo on Saturday at the harbour if you're interested." He took hold of an unwilling Jacob and turned away. "Come on. Back you go. Your teacher's going to kill you when she sees the state you're in."

The rest of the week passed in a confusion of new people, new places and new rules. At school, people eagerly discussed the ships that came and went, transferring oil from the crippled tanker to their own holds, but gradually the tanker story was slipping further down the headlines. As far as the rest of the world was concerned, it was no longer news.

On the last day of term, Tom and Beth headed

home, their pockets stuffed with information about healthy eating, how to tackle nits and a whole assortment of other trivia.

Mum met them on the doorstep. "Brian's back."

"We noticed." Tom was waiting for Beth to squeeze her way past the white van. This time it was parked right up against the door.

"He's turned the water off. Again," said Mum. "He says I need to go to the hardware shop and buy a reversible clip." She ran her fingers through her hair and stared at them, a little wildly. "What's a reversible clip?"

The children shrugged.

"It's going to be a while before tea then," said Tom, watching his mother as she struggled past the van and hurried down the street.

Beth sighed. "I never thought I'd say this," she said, "but I'm getting really sick of takeaways."

The clip failed to do the job. And later that night, Toby disgraced himself by soaking a wall plug, plunging the whole house into darkness. The only source of light was the gas cooker, so they all sat in the kitchen with the oven on and the door open, listening to the plink, plink, plink of water dripping from a leaky tap into the sink. Even making a cup of tea involved boiling a saucepan of water.

"It could be worse," Tom said the next morning. "I'm not playing football yet, but Connor always says hello."

"At least somebody's talking to you." Beth slumped across her bowl of corn flakes. It didn't taste very good because there was no electricity for the fridge and the milk was slightly warm. "The girls just giggle all the time. Most of them won't put a foot wrong in case they upset Mrs Ferguson. Except for the one with the fringe down to her nose. She just stares at you through a curtain of hair. It's creepy."

Breakfast was interrupted when Brian arrived, bringing an electrician along with him. Mum and Dad spent the morning guiding them round the house while they pointed out things that needed to be fixed, things that were urgent and things that were potentially lethal. Tom and Beth were ordered to make sure Toby stayed in the kitchen.

"Look!" Beth pointed at the window.

Tom followed his sister's finger just in time to see a woman in a red bobble hat walking briskly past the house. "Isn't that the woman from the POP meeting? I bet she's heading for the demonstration at the harbour."

"Let's go then." Beth jumped to her feet. "Anything's better than sitting around here."

"Where are you off to?" Mum arrived in the hall as they were pulling on their outdoor clothes. She was holding what the children had begun to think of as "THE NOTEBOOK."

"Just down to the harbour," said Tom. "There's a protest meeting about the oil tanker."

"Take the dog," said Mum, turning to a fresh page and beginning to scribble frantically.

"Do we have to?" Taking Toby into a crowd of people didn't seem a particularly good idea.

Mum didn't bother to look up. "Yes," she said. "You have to. I've got too much to do here to have him round my feet."

Chapter 6

Blue skies and sunshine had brought out a host of visitors. Most of them had come for a look at the tanker, but both Tom and Beth were surprised to see some of them settling down for an afternoon at the beach.

"I suppose it's a nice day for the seaside," said Beth doubtfully. "Except for that." She pointed towards the Bass and the tanker. Another ship lay alongside, connected to it by a long, dark tube.

"Look!" Tom tugged at Beth's sleeve. "Isn't that Connor's dad? And Jacob?"

A group of people had gathered in the open space in front of the Sea Bird Centre. Connor's dad was kneeling in front of a brightly coloured box, while Jacob jiggled impatiently from foot to foot beside him. A stream of iridescent bubbles flew out of the box and Jacob jumped up and down, whooping with triumph whenever he burst a bubble. The woman in the hat was beside him. She was watching the crowd, her eyes flicking constantly from one person to another.

"That's got to be POP," said Tom.

"Look over there." Beth pointed to a huge, whale-shaped balloon floating serenely above the harbour.

"Hi!"

They turned to find Connor standing behind them. Tom searched his mind for something interesting to say while Toby strained towards Connor, tongue lolling in a wide doggy smile.

Finally, Tom said, "There's a lot of people here."

Beth sniggered. Tom blushed, but Connor was too busy scratching Toby under the chin to notice. A helicopter clattered by overhead and they all tilted their heads to look.

"That's the coastguard," said Connor. "They're keeping an eye out in case anyone does something stupid."

"You mean something *more* stupid than risking an oil spill?"

All three turned to see a pirate in a three-cornered hat, with a patch over one eye and a huge golden hoop dangling from his ear.

Connor laughed. "Great costume, Danny!"

"Thanks, Connor." The pirate looked down at Toby. "Nice patch," he said as he moved on, "but the rest of my outfit's better than yours."

"Is that POP over there?" Tom nodded at the bubble machine.

"Yes," said Connor, "but there're lots of other people here too. The people with the whale balloon are from Friends of the Earth. And that big boat with the rainbow flag belongs to Greenpeace."

"It looks more like a party than a protest," said Beth.

"It's all about getting noticed," said Connor. "And it works." He pointed to where the film crew that Tom and Beth had seen last Sunday, were setting up their equipment. "We'll be on the national news again tonight for sure."

"That lot over there look like they're taking it a bit more seriously," said Tom. A group of people dressed in black wetsuits were sitting in a row, their legs dangling over the sea wall. The black suits had skeleton bones painted on them.

"That's Surfers against Slicks," said Connor.

"What about them?" Beth was looking at a man standing outside the Sea Bird Centre, cradling a small drum in the crook of his arm. He had long twisty dreadlocks dangling down to his shoulders. The girl beside him had bright green hair standing up in spikes all over her head. She waved cheerfully in their direction. Beth grinned and waved back.

"Those are the Eco-warriors," said Connor.

"And what about those two? Do they belong to POP as well?" Tom had spotted two men standing on the edge of the crowd, looking uncomfortably hot in their dark suits. One of them was mopping his forehead with a white handkerchief.

"Dunno," said Connor. "I've never seen them before."

"We have," said Beth. "We saw them coming out of the meeting last Saturday."

Connor shrugged. "Maybe they're supposed to be oil barons."

Beth frowned. "Maybe they really are oil barons."

"Don't think so," said Connor. "I don't think we're important enough for them to come to one of our meetings."

But Beth wasn't listening any more. She lifted her head and sniffed the air. "I smell food!"

"Over there!" She pointed to a huge oil drum near the beach steps. The top had been covered with wire mesh and converted into a barbecue. After this morning's meagre breakfast, the smell wafting towards her was irresistible. Beth stuck Toby's lead into Tom's hand.

"Hold on to him. I'll be back in a minute."

Tom and Connor watched her elbow her way purposefully through the crowd. There was another silence.

"Do you like football?" Connor said at last.

"Yes." Tom tried to sound casual. "I used to play at my other school."

"On the team?" Connor's eyes lit up.

For a moment Tom was tempted to stretch the truth. But he knew he would regret it later. "No," he admitted. "But I was a substitute."

"We play in the park most mornings," said Connor. "Maybe I'll see you there?"

Tom nodded casually.

Connor glanced across at the bubble machine. "I've got to go now. I have to keep an eye on Jacob."

Tom felt a huge smile spread across his face as he watched Connor walk away. "Come on, Toby," he said. "Let's go find Beth."

The man with the barbecue handed Beth her second hot dog and watched as she wolfed it down. "When did you last eat?"

"Breakfast, "said Beth, " … but it feels like forever." She sighed happily as she scattered the last pieces of the roll on to the sea wall for the birds.

"You shouldn't have done that," said a voice behind her.

Beth turned and came face to face with a giant puffin. It stared at her, an amused gleam in its eye.

"Why not?"

The question was barely out of her mouth before a horde of seagulls descended in a blinding storm of snapping beaks and whirling wings, each one determined to snatch a share of the crumbs. Beth turned in a circle, waving her arms wildly to drive them away, then as suddenly as they appeared, they were gone, leaving her gasping and dishevelled.

"Told you."

There was no doubt about it. The puffin was laughing at her. Beth frowned. Something about those eyes was familiar. So was the strand of dark brown hair peeking out from one eye-socket.

"You're in my class at school, aren't you?" Beth had to think hard before she came up with a name. "Elsie?"

The giant bird nodded.

"Why are you dressed up like that?"

The puffin attempted a shrug, but it didn't really have the shoulders for it. "Dad made me do it. That's him over there."

She waved a flipper at the pirate, who was now talking earnestly to the man with the drum.

"He runs the diving shop," said the puffin. "He said everyone else was too big for the costume and I didn't need to make a fuss because no one would know it was me."

Beth looked her up and down. "I like it."

The puffin laughed. "You're just saying that to make me feel better. But thanks anyway."

It turned and waddled away just as Tom arrived, hauling Toby along behind him.

"Who was that?"

"Elsie," Beth answered.

"You mean the girl with the face curtain?"

Beth scowled but Tom too intent on the barbecue to notice. "Did you get me anything to eat?"

"Not yet."

"Here. Take Toby."

A minute or two later, a roll on the drum signalled a general movement. Tom hurriedly stuffed the last of his hot dog into his mouth and followed Beth as people came together to form a circle with the drummer at the centre. The drummer took a bow and melted away, then Danny, the pirate, walked forward, leading Jacob by the hand.

He grinned. "A lot of you know me already, but for those who don't, my name is Danny McCall. I run the dive shop over ..." he waved in the direction of a small building across the road. "But I'm also a member of People against Pollution. We've spent years trying to get people to understand the danger of oil tankers using the river. And last Sunday proved we were right."

There was a loud chorus of agreement and another rattle on the drum. Danny held up a hand for silence.

"They tell us not to worry. They've got divers down there inspecting the damage and they're pumping out the oil, ship to ship." He shook his head slowly, his eyes travelling round the crowd. "But there are other things they're not telling us. They can't use ship to ship transfer on the damaged hold in case they dislodge the tanker from the rock." His face darkened. "That hold still contains thousands of tonnes of crude oil. We're only safe for as long as the weather holds. And there's more to worry about than the sea life that gets caught directly in the spill." He waved in the direction of the Bass Rock. "It's breeding season. There're millions of chicks out there. How are they going to survive without their parents to feed them?"

Jacob frowned and tugged at Danny's hand. Danny smiled down at him.

"This is such an important occasion that we thought someone ought to make a proper speech."

Everyone plastered a look of polite interest on their faces. The pirate grinned. "But then we decided that would be boring. So instead, Jacob here has offered to tell us why he likes the seaside."

Jacob gave a huge smile. There was another roll of the drum as he stepped forward, took a deep breath and began talking about how much he liked building sandcastles, and how the sand would be no good if it was all sticky and covered in oil.

Eventually Danny tapped him on the shoulder, but Jacob took another deep breath and carried on talking.

Beth yawned. Tom swallowed the last of his hot dog. Toby sighed and lay down beside him. Tom's eyes wandered to the edge of the crowd.

"Look Beth," he said. "There's the professor!"

Professor MacBlain was standing in the open doorway of the Sea Bird Centre, a look of total disbelief on his face. When he spotted the TV crew, his expression changed to one of horrified dismay.

The two children exchanged a puzzled glance as they watched the professor start to shuffle sideways towards the harbour steps.

"He doesn't seem very keen on joining in," said Tom.

"Professor MacBlain has his own ideas about how to go about things," said Mike's voice behind them.

The professor's attempt to escape unnoticed was not a success. As he began a cautious slither around the back of the crowd, the woman in the red bobble hat stepped out from between two skeletons and grabbed him firmly by the arm.

Chapter 7

The professor was trying to pull free, but it was obvious there was no way the woman was letting go. She leaned right into his face, talking intently, ignoring his increasingly desperate attempts to get away.

It was Jacob who gave the professor his opportunity to escape. Anxious to get things moving, Danny waved Mike forward, but his next words were drowned by Jacob's roar of outrage as his father lifted him up and carried him away. Jacob was determined not to give up without a fight. He struggled wildly in his father's arms, clutching at anyone within range in an effort to break free. Most people were giving him a wide berth, but the woman in the hat was too intent on the professor to notice. Crimson-faced with embarrassment, Mike finally made it to the edge of the crowd. Jacob reached out and grabbed hold of the woman, hanging on like a shipwrecked sailor clinging to a rock. The professor took advantage of the distraction to pull away and quickly disappeared from view.

"Come on," said Beth. "Let's find out what's going on!" She began to squeeze her way through the press of people, pulling Toby along behind her. With one regretful look at the barbecue Tom followed his sister out of the crowd.

By the time they caught up with him, the professor had reached the bottom of the harbour steps.

"Hallo!" Beth called but he didn't stop, just kept on moving so that they were forced to jog alongside, Toby trotting eagerly at their heels.

"I'm sorry," he said. "I can't talk now."

"But don't you want to join in the protest?" Beth was having a hard time trying to keep up without getting herself tangled in Toby's lead.

The professor stopped and turned to face them. "I didn't know about the meeting," he said. "I shouldn't have come here today. It was a mistake."

"Why?" Beth couldn't understand it. The professor had helped set up People Against Pollution, so why wouldn't he take part in the demonstration? It didn't make any sense.

Professor MacBlain's eyes drifted past Beth and she saw a look of horror appear on his face. "Perhaps it's already too late," he whispered.

"What is it?" asked Tom. "What's wrong?"

But the professor just turned and hurried away without answering. Toby whined in disappointment and tugged on the lead, unwilling to lose sight of his new friend.

"What was it? What did he see?" Beth turned to look behind her and was knocked to one side by the woman in the red bobble hat, who rushed on past without taking the time to apologise.

"Charming," said Beth, as Tom grabbed hold of her.

"Something is definitely going on," said Tom, a puzzled frown on his face.

"You're right," said Beth. "And we're going to find out what it is!"

Together they set off after the woman, round the side of the harbour and up on to the narrow concrete path that wound its way in and out of the rocks on the headland.

"He's not going to get away from her if he went this way," said Tom. "There's nothing out there but water."

Beth had no breath to answer him. Toby was now bounding ahead, dragging her along behind.

When they arrived at the end of the path, there was no sign of the professor. The only person they could see was the woman in the hat, staring out across the water. She turned round and saw the children.

"Did you see a man come along here?" she called. "Do you know where he went?"

"What man?" Tom tried for a look of innocent surprise.

"Professor MacBlain, of course," snapped the woman.

"What do you want him for?" asked Beth.

The woman frowned. "I don't think that's any of your business." She turned to the water. "There's no way off these rocks," she said. "And there's no sign of a boat. Unless..." she turned back to the children. "Have you seen ...?"

But they never got to hear the rest of it. Toby had enjoyed the chase tremendously and was delighted to find another new friend at the end of it. He leaped forward and Beth squeaked in dismay as the lead slid out of her sweaty grasp. The woman saw what was coming and put out both hands. But it did no good. Barking with excitement, Toby leaped forward and hit her squarely in the chest.

Horrified, the children watched as she teetered on the edge of the path, her arms flailing. She hung there for one awful moment and then suddenly she was gone.

"Oh no!" The children rushed forward. Hardly daring to look, they knelt down beside a confused-looking Toby and peered over the edge. Beth let out a gasp of relief. The woman was just below them, perched on a mossy rock like an enormous bird on its nest. She glared up at them, her face red with indignation.

"I'm so sorry," said Beth. "It was an accident ... I tried to hold on to the lead but he just got away from me."

"Never mind about the dog!" snapped the woman. She rocked from side to side, trying to get back on her feet. "Just get me out of here!"

"Is there anything wrong?"

The children jumped up and whirled round to find themselves face to face with the men in suits.

"Of course there's something wrong," came a bellow from below. "Get over here and help me up!"

The tall one moved forward and peered over the edge while the short man looked around. "Where is Professor MacBlain?"

"Never mind that!" The woman's patience had clearly run out. "Just get me back up!"

Tall suit looked hard at Beth and Tom. "You two wait there," he ordered, then he and his companion knelt down and reached out their hands to the woman below.

Tom bent and picked up the lead. For once, Toby

didn't make a fuss. He seemed to understand that he had done something truly awful.

"Can't we go, Tom?" Beth trembled at the thought of what the woman might say to her when she managed to clamber back up the rock.

Tom was clearly thinking the same thing. "Yeah … I don't think she needs our help, do you? She doesn't seem to be hurt. Just angry."

Beth shook her head. Already, the woman was slowly making her way up the rock, huffing and puffing with the effort. Quietly, the children turned and walked away, trying not to look as though they were in any particular hurry. They kept going until they had climbed off the headland and reached the harbour steps, where Tom stopped and looked back, chewing his lip like he always did when he was nervous.

"Maybe we should have stayed," he said.

"Don't be daft!" said Beth. "Didn't you see her face? She was absolutely furious."

"She might have been hurt," said Tom.

"No she wasn't! It was only a little way down. She didn't even lose her hat." Beth started up the steps. "And anyway," she added over her shoulder. "It wasn't our fault, not really."

Tom gritted his teeth and began climbing the steps, Toby following obediently at his heels.

Beth stopped. "All right," she said. "It was my fault. I should have held on tighter."

Tom felt a twinge of sympathy at the misery in her voice. "Well, I suppose it was really Toby's fault." He cast another nervous glance behind him and started moving again. "But he *is* our dog."

"I think this must be my worst week ever," mumbled Beth as she trailed up the steps and into the welcoming anonymity of the crowd.

Chapter 8

"I wish we'd never moved here." Beth was in the kitchen along with the rest of the family. There wasn't much point in being anywhere else.

The electrician had warned them to use nothing except the lights, in case they blew a fuse or even worse, set the house on fire. That meant no TV, no computer, no electrical anything. A battery-powered radio sat on the table, with voices murmuring softly to each other, like a conversation in another room, but no one was really listening to it. Toby lay on the floor in front of the open oven door, snoring loudly. Every so often, he would give a whuffling sigh and turn his body round to warm up a different bit.

Since neither Beth nor Tom had mentioned the disaster at the harbour, Dad thought she was just talking about life in general.

"Give it time," he said. "You can't make friends overnight."

"It's all right for Tom," Beth grumbled, sliding her toes under Toby's body. "At least he's got someone to play football with."

Tom had dredged up some Lego from somewhere and was trying to build a spaceship, even though half the bits were missing. "You're not entirely on your own, Beth. You've got the girl with the face curtain."

"Elsie," snapped Beth. "Her name is Elsie!"

Mum shifted in her chair and raised her head from her notebook. "I think this is nice. It's not often we spend an evening together. You'll get to know people eventually, Beth. And look at what we've got in exchange ... a house with real character, right beside the harbour. The attic bedrooms even have a view of the sea."

"A view of the tanker more like," muttered Beth.

"You can't see out unless you stand on tiptoe on a chair," added Tom. "And we haven't even got proper beds to sleep in."

"At least you've both got a room of your own," countered Mum. When she saw their mouths open she added hastily, "Well ... you will have when the broken window's fixed. We've even got a garden!"

"No we haven't," said Beth. "Just a concrete backyard with a wheelie bin and one of those twirly clothes dryers."

"That's not what I see when I look out there." Mum's eyes took on a faraway look.

"Come on, kids," Dad closed the book he was reading and looked from Tom to Beth. "You always used to like coming here to Grannie's caravan."

"For a *week*," said Tom.

"In the *summer*," added Beth.

"This *is* the summer." Dad's normally laidback voice was deepening into a growl. He hated arguments. "And your mother's right. Just think of what you've got here compared to town."

"We've got creaky floorboards, draughty windows and no heating," said Tom. "And everything leaks."

The drip of water into the kitchen sink under-scored his words.

Mum sighed. "I admit this isn't how I planned it. But I don't have time for normal things right now. You're just going to have to be patient. We'll get things sorted out, I promise."

Everyone cringed as she reached for the note-book, clearly intent on listing all of the things that needed doing or had already been done. They were saved by a knock at the front door.

"That'll be the builder," said Mum, leaping to her feet.

But it wasn't. When the kitchen door opened. Tom and Beth froze in surprise to see a tubby fig-ure standing in the doorway. Toby jumped up and hurried over to say hello.

The professor bent and scratched the top of Toby's head. "Hallo there." He looked up with an apologetic smile. "I'm sorry to interrupt, but I just wondered if I could have a quick word with the children." He took off his hat and wiped his glis-tening forehead.

Tom frowned, wondering how the professor knew where they lived. Then he leaned over and gave Beth a nudge. "You put our address in the visitor's book, didn't you?"

"Have they done something wrong?" Dad asked.

"Not at all, not at all," said the professor. "Quite the opposite. Allow me to introduce myself," he said. "I am Professor Angus MacBlain. Your children, Tom and er … Beth, came to my little demonstra-tion at the Jubilee Hall the Saturday before last."

"You're a professor?" Dad was trying to get a handle on who this strange little man might be.

"Yes," said the professor. "At Waverley University. I work on marine life — in particular the waters of the Firth of Forth. We're very keen to get young people involved in our project. I have my card here somewhere." After a few moments rummaging, he produced a creased and grubby cardboard square.

Dad took it and looked down with a puzzled frown. "Has this got anything to do with the tanker?"

"Not quite!" The professor gave a nervous cough. "Tom and Beth expressed an interest in my work and I thought they might like to find out a little more about it."

"Well ..." said Dad. He glanced at Mum, who was surreptitiously leafing through her notebook. "I suppose it's not a problem, is it Gwen?"

Mum looked up briefly. "I suppose not."

The professor took another deep breath. "I only need a quick word and I can see you're both busy. Perhaps you have somewhere else where I wouldn't be in your way?"

"You could use the living room," Dad said doubtfully. "But it's not very nice in there at the moment."

"Not a problem," said the professor eagerly.

Tom looked at Beth, but she looked just as puzzled as he was. Together, they led the way to the sitting room at the front of the house. Tom reached out and switched on the light ... a little nervously, thanks to the electrician's dire warnings. The room was crowded with various belongings, all waiting to be unpacked. It smelt odd; a combination of apples and toast and lavender polish, not bad smells on their own but somehow unsettling all together, like a ghostly echo of someone else's life.

They barely had time to shut the door before the professor turned to them with a look of desperation on his face. "I need your help!" He squeezed past a pile of boxes and lifted the net curtain to peer out the window.

Tom frowned. "Is this about that woman?"

The professor dropped the curtain and looked round. "What woman?"

"You know," said Beth. "The one in the red bobble hat. You were talking to her this afternoon."

The professor shook his head and began wringing his hands. "They're closing in," he said. "I have to move ... but I can't do it by myself!"

"Move?"

"Someplace safe." His eyes jumped between them. "Will you help me?"

"But Professor," said Tom patiently, "we don't know what you want our help *with.*"

"And I don't see why you picked us," said Beth.

The professor's face darkened. "Because you're the only ones who are interested. Everyone around here thinks I'm mad." He attempted a feeble smile. "But I'm not, you know. And it's not dangerous – well, not really. I only need a few hours of your time."

The conversation was going round and round and getting nowhere.

"Look," said Tom. "You can't expect us to help if you ..."

But the professor was no longer listening. He was peering through the net curtain.

The sound of another knock at the door made the children jump. The professor dropped the curtain and turned round, a look of desperation on his face.

"I have to get out of here."

"It's probably just the builder," said Beth.

"I have to get away!"

Beth gave up. "You can go out the back," she said. "There's a door in the wall that leads into the lane."

The professor was down the corridor and away before the front door opened. They heard Mum's voice, followed by a deeper rumble.

"Well," said Tom "I don't know who the professor was expecting. But one thing's for sure. It definitely wasn't the builder."

Chapter 9

"Who *is* that woman in the red bobble hat?" asked Beth as she switched off her torch and unzipped her sleeping bag. She was wearing an overstretched t-shirt and a pair of bright green tracksuit bottoms. Ugly, but comfy for sleeping in. There wasn't much choice anyway, now that the washing machine was out of action.

"And don't forget those two men in suits." She clambered inside the bag and pulled up the zip. "Maybe they're spies for an oil company?" She raised her eyebrows, forgetting it was too dark for Tom to see her.

"Just listen to yourself," scoffed Tom. "You'd think you were in the middle of a James Bond movie."

"Connor's dad said the professor had a different approach to things." Her voice was thoughtful. "Maybe he's not interested in peaceful protests." She sat up suddenly, switched on her torch and shone it in Tom's face. "Maybe he's going to blow up the tanker!"

"Don't be so silly, Beth." Tom raised a hand to shield his face. "They want to stop oil escaping into the river. Why on earth would the professor want to blow it up?"

"Well, something's going on," insisted Beth. "I'm not imagining that."

"No," said Tom. "You're not." He frowned. "But

we can't ask Professor MacBlain. We don't have any idea where he is." He lowered his hand. "I suppose we could try the university. Dad's got his card, hasn't he?"

"It's no good," said Beth. "I already phoned the number."

"When?" Tom sat up and looked at her in surprise

"While Mum and Dad were talking to the builder. But it just says the number is disconnected."

"Then why did he give us the card?" asked Tom.

"He didn't," Beth pointed out. "He gave it to Dad." She switched off the torch and snuggled back into the bag. "I expect he was just trying to make himself look official, so Mum and Dad would let him talk to us."

Tom yawned and lay down. "I suppose he's not going to answer the phone if he doesn't want anyone to find him."

"Then we're stuck, aren't we?" said Beth.

"We could go back to Jubilee Hall," said Tom. "He wouldn't just leave all that stuff there, would he? He must keep an eye on it."

They arrived at the hall on Sunday morning just as Jacob tumbled out the door, dragging Connor along behind him.

"Got to take him to the park," he yelled as he flew past Tom and Beth. "See you tomorrow, Tom."

Tom nodded and gave him a thumbs-up.

"What are you doing tomorrow?" Beth asked.

"Playing football." Tom gave Beth a sympathetic glance. "Sorry."

Beth shrugged and moved on purposefully, but when she and Tom reached the foot of the basement steps, they were faced with a firmly closed door

"Great!" Beth ground her teeth in frustration.

"We could maybe go and talk to Connor's dad," said Tom. "He might know where to find him."

"It's Sunday," she reminded him. "The Hall's closed on a Sunday."

She grabbed the door handle and let go in surprise as it turned in her hand. The door swung slowly open, to reveal a dark and silent interior.

"There's got to be a light switch somewhere." Beth reached up and fumbled for a moment before the dingy strip light went on. The little table had disappeared, but the rest of the basement was the same — a wasteland of broken furniture and mysterious, lumpy objects hidden beneath grubby sheets.

Together, they crossed the room. Beth reached out and pulled the cover off the aquarium, but there was nothing inside apart from a thin scattering of sand on the bottom and a solitary mussel still stuck to the glass.

"The wardrobe!" She hurried over to the corner, but when she pulled on the handle, the wardrobe door swung open to reveal an ordinary, water-stained and warped interior. There was no conveyor belt, no wires or tubes and no fuel cell.

Beth turned in a slow circle. "It's all gone," she said. "Everything's gone. He's cleared it all out." She frowned at Tom.

"He told us to come back," said Tom thought-fully, "So he must have meant to leave it here. Something must have happened to make him change his mind."

The basement suddenly grew darker. They exchanged a look, then turned round to see two familiar figures blocking the light from the door-way.

"Well, well." Tall Suit began to walk towards them. "You two seem to pop up everywhere. But you don't seem very keen on hanging around for long, do you?"

Beth clutched Tom's arm. It felt like judgement day had arrived. "We were only looking for Professor MacBlain," she quavered.

Short Suit followed his partner across the empty space. Both of them stared down at the children as though they were looking at something interesting under a microscope.

"That's a coincidence," said Tall Suit. "So are we."

Tom shifted a little, wishing Beth would loosen her grip. She was squeezing so tight his arm had gone numb. "Why are you looking for him?"

"That's not important," said Short Suit. "Has Professor MacBlain been here recently?"

"Why are you looking for him?" Beth repeated, feeling braver now that she knew it wasn't her or Tom the men were after, but the missing profes-sor.

Tall Suit tutted. "Has no one ever told you it's rude to answer a question with a question?" He frowned down at the children. "Professor

MacBlain has something that does not belong to him. We have been asked to find it. Our client is very anxious to have it back."

"We don't know anything about that," said Beth. "We've only met the professor a couple of times. And I don't think he's been here in ages. All his stuff's gone."

Somehow, neither Tom nor Beth felt inclined to mention the professor's visit to their house.

Short Suit took over. "I think you know the professor a little better than that," he said. "You seemed very anxious to have a word with him at the protest meeting."

"We just wanted to say hello," said Tom. "We met him at one of his demonstrations. We don't really know anything about him at all."

"Well," said Tall Suit smoothly, "if you hear from him again, you will let us know, won't you?"

He pulled something from his pocket and took a step forward. Tom and Beth couldn't help taking a step back. He smiled. It wasn't a particularly nice smile.

"Here's my card."

Tom reached out and took it. Unlike the professor's, this one was white, square edged and crisp.

"Come along, Henry. Let's go. And remember ..." Tall Suit waved a finger at the children. "If you hear from the professor at all, it would be very wise to tell us."

The two men walked away, leaving Tom and Beth alone in the basement.

Beth looked at her brother. "Henry?"

They stared at each other for a moment, and

then, hysterical with relief, they laughed until they cried.

"That was scary," Beth said at last, wiping her eyes on her sleeve.

"Let's get out of here," said Tom. "They might change their minds and come back."

Suddenly anxious once again, they hurried towards the door and didn't stop until they reached the end of the alley and were back on the street.

"Looks like we've lost track of the professor for good," said Tom. "And to tell you the truth, I'm not really sorry." He shivered, remembering those two looming figures in the dark basement.

"Can I see that card?" Beth asked.

Tom handed it over.

"Barratt and Maclean. Professional Investigations," she read. "Private and discreet." She looked at Tom. "What does discreet mean?"

He shrugged. "I think it just means private."

"Then why do they say it twice?" She tapped the card thoughtfully against her teeth. "I wonder who their client is. And what has the professor got that they want? It can't be the dog walker."

"I don't know," said Tom as they headed for the chip shop. "But I do know one thing."

"What?"

"Things around here are getting odder and odder."

Chapter 10

Next morning, Tom arrived at the park to discover that almost everyone else was there before him.

"Last person to get here is the goalie," explained Connor. "You play for one team in the first half then we change sides and you're in the same goal, but for the other team. We're still waiting for Alex, but he won't be going in goal. He's too good."

Alex appeared as Tom was still plodding across the field and the game began even before he reached the goal. Not that it mattered, because he was at the opposite end of the field from all the action. He leaned against the goalpost and settled in for a long wait. In some ways it was a relief, but it was also extremely boring.

Connor was right. Alex would have been wasted in goal. He was miles faster than everyone else and he knew what to do with the ball when he got it. By the time they changed ends, Connor's team was three-nil down.

There was a brief flurry after the kick off and for once, Connor managed to send the ball down towards the other end. But Alex was on to it as soon as it landed and wove his way back up the pitch, neatly evading everyone who tried to take the ball away from him.

He was coming fast, but Tom was ready for him. He leaped forward in what should have been a perfect save and was already in the air when he saw the look of triumph on his opponent's face. The ball went straight into the corner of the net and Tom crashed heavily to the ground.

The rest of his team were furious and not afraid to say so. Only Connor stood up for him.

"Never mind," he said, giving Tom a friendly slap on the back. "The goalie always gets the blame."

When he finally unlocked the front door and limped back into the kitchen, he found Beth sitting at the table, flipping idly through the pages of a book and feeding Toby forbidden snacks.

"Mum and Dad have gone to the bank," she said. "How was your football game?"

"Terrible." Tom dropped into a chair. "I let in three goals."

"Isn't that what it's all about?" Beth pushed a packet of biscuits in his direction. "Getting the ball in the net?"

"Very funny." Tom took a biscuit and munched without enthusiasm.

"Well, I had a great time!" Beth's eyes were sparkling. "I went to the harbour and helped Elsie load up her dad's boat. He said I can maybe go out with them some time, but not till the tanker's dealt with. Elsie gave me this book. It's a bit scary. Listen …"

Ignoring the fact that Tom didn't seem to be paying attention, she flicked backwards and forwards through the book till she found the right page, then began to read.

"*Environmental damage depends on the type of oil and the size of the spill. Surface oil will evaporate eventually or sink, or be washed on to the shore. Some will ... "* she broke off and sniffed, her nose crinkling in disgust, then looked down at Toby in horror.

"It's not Toby," said Tom miserably. "It's me. I fell in a pile of dog's muck. And I didn't even save the goal."

Beth laughed. "Never mind. Elsie's dad paid me for helping out." She waved a ten-pound note under Tom's nose. "And you can help me spend it!"

Tom gave his sister a quavery smile. One thing about Beth, she was always ready to share. The good things as well as the bad.

After a quick wash and a change of clothes, Tom followed Beth into the street, still struggling to get his arm into the sleeve of his jacket. "What's the hurry?"

"I want to get to the library before it closes for lunch," said Beth.

"What for?" Tom was puzzled. Beth's interest in books had expanded lately, due to a lack of anything else to do, but she wasn't all that enthusiastic about reading.

"I want to check my e-mail," she said. "Elsie told me they've got computers there. I can talk to people online. Assuming I've still got any friends left."

"Did Elsie say anything about the professor?"

"Yes," said Beth. "She doesn't know where he lives, but he's been around for ever. He's got some kind of project going with the university, but she didn't know much about that either. Did you ask Connor?"

"I didn't get a chance," said Tom defensively.

Beth soon discovered that every workstation in the library was occupied. She wandered disconsolately back to Tom, clutching a leaflet about how to join the library.

"The lady at the desk says it's always busy during the school holidays. If I make a booking, then I can have a space on Thursday. But I don't want to wait till Thursday."

Very slowly Tom reached out for his sister and drew her behind a bookshelf.

"She's here," he whispered.

"Who?" Beth peered round the corner of the shelf.

The woman in the red hat was unloading a pile of books from a wicker basket on to the counter. Beth ducked back as the woman turned to survey the room.

"Do you think she knows where the professor is?"

"I don't know," said Tom. "But she's the only clue we've got. What do you think? Should we keep an eye on where she goes?"

Beth screwed up her face, unable to make up her mind. "What if she sees me? She'll remember it was me who let Toby jump on her."

"I was there too," Tom pointed out.

"And what about Mum? She told us to be sure and not forget to bring back a measuring tape."

Tom knew that was only an excuse. Beth was always quick to rush into any situation, but she wasn't really all that brave. She definitely didn't want to come face to face with the woman in the hat.

"Okay," he said. "You get the tape and take it home. Get yourself a baseball cap or something. She probably won't recognise us without Toby. I'll keep an eye on where she goes. Phone me when you get to the house and I'll tell you where I am." He frowned in thought. "No. That's a bad idea. She might hear the phone ring. I'll call you. Just wait till then."

Beth looked at him in admiration. "You're pretty good at this, aren't you?"

Tom shrugged. "I just hope I'm a better tracker than a goalie." He risked another peek round the bookshelf. "She's leaving," he said. "I'll see you later."

The tape measure safely delivered, Beth found herself a hat and then hung around, ready to leap into action as soon as the phone rang.

"She's just come out of the baker's," said Tom's voice in her ear.

"What did she buy?"

Beth heard a deep sigh from the other end of the phone.

"What difference does that make? I'm trying to keep an eye on her, not find out what buns she likes."

"Sorry," said Beth. "I got carried away. See you in a minute."

"When will you be back?" called Mum as she was heading for the door. "Toby needs a walk."

"Not sure, Mum," Beth called back. "We might

see Elsie … or Connor." She shut the door quickly behind her, telling herself that it wasn't a lie. It *was* possible they would see them. She hadn't said they were going to spend any time with them.

She spotted Tom across the High Street, walking slowly towards her. The woman in the bobble hat was a little way in front of him. Beth walked quickly past on the other side of the street then crossed the road and hurried to catch up with Tom.

"Do you know where she's going?"

"I'm not a mind reader, Beth," said Tom crossly. "Just keep quiet. Walk slowly and be ready to dive for cover if I tell you."

"She's heading for the sea," Beth hissed in Tom's ear. He nodded. The woman turned down their street. They waited a few moments, then turned to follow, halting abruptly as they saw her standing at the end of the road. If she turned around now there was no way she wouldn't see them.

But she didn't turn. Instead she pulled something from her basket, frowned down at it and then carried on across the road, moving more briskly than before.

"Not the beach," said Beth. "She's going back to the harbour."

The oil drum barbecue was still there, with a few diehard demonstrators still clustered around it. One of them smiled as the children hurried past. "Have you come to keep us company?"

"Maybe later," said Tom. "There's something we have to do first."

"Come on," said Beth. "We'll lose her!"

"I don't think so," said Tom, following his sister. "There's no place for her to go except the headland."

Cautiously, they followed, peering round each rock before moving any further along the path. Eventually, they stuck their heads round a particularly large boulder and found themselves face to face with the woman they had been following.

She blinked at them. They blinked back. Slowly, they emerged from the shelter of the rock. There was no point in trying to pretend they weren't there.

"You two again!" Her eyes narrowed. "I hope you haven't got that dog with you."

"No," said Tom. "We're on our own."

"Is that so?" She tilted her head and looked at them.

She had very piercing grey eyes. Beth edged a little further behind her brother.

"Have you seen Professor MacBlain?" The woman stepped forward eagerly.

"Professor MacBlain?" Tom tried to sound surprised.

The woman stepped closer, her eyes flinty. "I saw you talking to him on Saturday," she said. "Don't pretend you don't know him."

"No," Tom said hastily. "We haven't seen him. Not lately, anyway."

It occurred to Beth that they were both getting rather good at bending the truth.

"He's around here somewhere," the woman said thoughtfully. "He must be." She glanced around again, then looked back at the children. "If you see him, it's important that you let me know."

The two children nodded eagerly.

"Good. You can get in touch with me through POP. The folk round the fire will give you the number."

They nodded again, as she walked past them and disappeared round the bend in the path. Then they turned and looked at each other. Beth opened her mouth, but before she could say anything a familiar voice spoke from somewhere near their feet.

"Thank God she's gone."

Chapter 11

Tom moved to the edge of the path and peered over. "Professor MacBlain," he said. "What are you doing down there?"

The professor was standing on a shelf of rock just a few steps below them. "I need your help," he called. "They're closing in." He gestured impatiently. "Hurry up! I can't hang around here. She might come back."

Tom looked down at the professor, then glanced uncertainly at his sister.

Beth nodded eagerly. "Go on," she urged.

One behind the other, the children clambered down to join the professor. It was an easy climb; almost as though the stones had been shaped into a set of rough steps. And the rock at the bottom was more than wide enough for all three of them.

Tom shifted to one side to make room on the ledge for Beth. He looked around dubiously. The water was well below them, but the clumps of damp seaweed and the barnacles clinging to the rocks made it obvious that this was not always the case.

Close up, they could see that the professor was unshaven and bleary-eyed. He was still wearing his shorts, but he had swapped his shirt for a heavy fisherman's jersey that didn't look as if it had ever been washed. "Don't worry about the water," he said. "The tide is right out." He gave a brief glance at the waves lapping gently against the rocks below. "It'll turn soon, but we've still got plenty of time."

"What for?" Beth asked.

But the professor wasn't interested in any more conversation. With a curt, "Follow me," he moved to one side of the ledge, pushed aside a dangling curtain of seaweed and forced his way through a gap in the rocks barely wide enough to accommodate his tubby body.

Ignoring her brother's doubtful frown, Beth crossed the ledge and slipped through the gap, leaving him no choice but to follow. Tom emerged from behind the smelly, damp curtain to find Beth alone on another ledge. Somehow the professor had managed to repeat his disappearing trick

"Where is he now?"

"He went in there." Beth pointed to the wall of rock.

Tom turned to look. Instead of solid stone, the barnacles and the seaweed were attached to an iron grille, its bars pitted, corroded and streaked with rust.

A heavy iron padlock was fixed to the iron bars but when Beth took hold of it, it swung loose in her hand. "It's not locked, Tom." She pulled harder and the grille swung slowly open. A gust of dank, seaweedy air puffed out of the hole.

Tom peered into the dark space. There was still no sign of the professor.

"If he can get in there, then there must be plenty room for us." Before Tom could say or do anything to stop her, Beth ducked her head and walked forward into the darkness. And, like the professor before her, she simply disappeared.

"Beth!" Tom called her name, quietly at first, then louder. "Beth! Come back!" He narrowed his eyes, trying to catch a glimpse of movement from within, but there was nothing.

He heard a faint, muffled shout and strained his ears to listen. The noise came again and he realized Beth was calling him from somewhere deep inside the rock. Taking a deep breath, he walked into the gap, fighting a wave of claustrophobia as the cave walls narrowed about him.

In only a few short steps he came up against a wall of solid rock, but his reaching fingers told him there was empty space off to one side. Gathering his courage, he took a sideways step, and found himself in a much wider tunnel that smelt of dust and decaying seaweed. He was surprised to discover that it wasn't dark. Instead, the walls were bathed in a soft green light.

"That must be the luminous moss." Beth was right in front of him, staring at the glowing patches that spread all over the walls and the roof, bathing the nooks and crannies with soft green light. But Tom looked down at the puddles at his feet and frowned.

"I don't think this place is very safe, Beth," he said, and shivered at the thought of what it would be like to be trapped in here when the water was rising.

The professor was standing just a short way ahead. A smile spread across his face. "I'm very glad you decided to join me. I'm absolutely sure you won't regret it." The smile widened as he watched their faces. "It's an old smugglers' tunnel," he said. "Useful, don't you think?"

"So that's how you did your disappearing trick," said Beth softly.

Tom stared around, his worries momentarily forgotten. A genuine, honest-to-goodness smugglers' tunnel!

"Beth," he whispered. "This must have been here for hundreds of years."

"Don't worry," said the professor, dragging him back to reality. "It only floods during really high tides."

Tom looked at him suspiciously. "I think we've probably come as far as we should," he said.

"Let me ask you a question, Tom." The professor tilted his head and looked at him. "This moss ... would you say it's natural here?"

"I dunno ... maybe." Tom had never seen anything like it before he met the professor, but that didn't mean much.

The professor reached out and ran his hand down the soft green covering on the wall. "Well it isn't. I brought this here and encouraged it to grow. It's not native, but I wanted a biologically based light source." His eyes still twinkled, but they suddenly looked a lot sharper. "You told me you care about the environment. But you don't know enough to care. What I'm offering you is the chance to learn." He turned away, his voice floating back towards the children. "And believe me, you won't regret taking up my offer."

"Beth," said Tom slowly. "I think we should go back."

"No!" Her voice sent echoes bouncing off the walls. She turned to face him. "He's got something hidden down here. Something important! Don't you want to know what it is?"

It was hard to think sensibly with Beth huffing and puffing impatiently and the professor moving further and further away, but Tom had to admit Beth was right. He did want to know. And from the look of the moss that covered the walls, the professor had been using this tunnel for quite a while without coming to any harm. "All right!" he said at last. "We'll go just a little further. And then we stop."

"I'm glad you said that," said Beth. "Because I was going to follow him anyway."

Tom didn't believe her. He didn't think she was brave enough to face a walk through the tunnel with only the professor for company. She set off down the tunnel and he followed after her, trying not to think about where this might lead them. If anything went wrong, it would be both of them who ended up in trouble, not just Beth.

"We still don't know who that woman is," he said as he hurried along, keeping an anxious eye on the distant figure of Professor MacBlain.

"She told us to get in touch with her through POP," said Beth, "but that could be just a front, couldn't it? I still think she's working undercover. Maybe with those two men."

Tom didn't want to think about the men in suits. They were far too sinister. "Well," he said, "Whoever she is, she's determined to track down the professor. And he's just as determined to keep out of her way."

They stopped for a minute to catch their breath. Beth saw Tom glance uneasily at the stone roof.

"It can't be much further," she said with an encouraging smile. "We must be nearly at the harbour. Isn't this amazing?"

Tom didn't smile back. "Mum and Dad must be wondering where we are."

"Well, give them a call," said Beth. "You've got your phone."

"I don't think I'll get a signal under all this rock."

"Don't worry about it, then." Beth increased her steps in an effort to catch up with the professor, who was moving awfully fast for such a tubby little man.

"We can't get lost," she said. "There're no side tunnels. And look." She pointed ahead. "He's stopped."

She was right. The professor was waiting a little way in front of them, red-faced and out of breath. As they came closer, they could hear the sound of water lapping against stone.

"Journey's end," he said when they caught up. "They say this tunnel used to go all the way to the ruined church near the Sea Bird Centre, but that was before they widened the harbour and built a new wall."

He was standing at the entrance to a little cave. Tom peered past him and saw that the tunnel came to an end in a solid stone wall covered in a dripping mass of green slime.

"You were right Beth," he said over his shoulder. "We're right up against the harbour wall."

He wondered what was waiting for them in this long abandoned space. Whatever it was, he didn't think it would be chests filled with treasure or piles of gold doubloons.

The cave was almost circular, with sandy edges sloping gently down to a pool of water. Pieces of discarded equipment lay all around, littering the sand. Tom began to walk forward, his eyes wandering across pieces of plastic tubing and piles of cogs and wheels and springs. The conveyor belt from the dog walker was dumped in one corner. Finally, he focused on the pool in the centre of the cave and stopped dead.

"Unbelievable." His incredulous whisper floated back towards Beth. The indoor dog walker had not prepared him for anything like this.

"What? What is it? Let me see!" Beth pushed and squeezed her way past her brother. Her jaw dropped and her eyes widened in awestruck wonder as she stared at the shape floating on the surface of the pool.

At last she found her voice. "A submarine," she gasped. "You stole a submarine."

Chapter 12

The professor's heavy eyebrows came down in a ferocious frown. "I stole nothing! This is my project! I got the money together." He slapped his chest. "I built her! Me! She wouldn't exist if it wasn't for me ... the university doesn't own her. Nobody owns her. She belongs with me!"

Neither Tom nor Beth answered. They were mesmerised by the sight of the oval shape floating just below them. It was clearly a submarine, but nothing like any submarine either of them had ever imagined. They could see right though the grey, cigar-shaped body. The space inside glowed with a soft, blue light that seemed to come from everywhere all at once. It looked more like a spaceship than anything made on earth.

"It's beautiful," whispered Beth.

"Very, very cool indeed," said Tom in a low voice. He couldn't take his eyes off it. "How come we can see inside? What's it made of?"

The professor smiled, his anger subsiding in the face of their admiration. "This is the world's first fully bio-friendly submersible. She has a clear perspex body made from recycled plastic. Her name is Gaia ..."

"I've heard about Gaia!" Beth tore her eyes from the submarine. "It's a word for everything that lives on Earth, isn't it?"

The professor gave an approving nod. "Not bad,

Beth. Not bad at all. Gaia was a goddess first, the mother of all the earth. But nowadays, scientists use her name to describe how the whole earth works together as a single, living organism."

"A living organism?" Beth looked back at the submarine, her eyes soft with wonder. "Does that mean Gaia's ... alive?"

"Alive?" The professor raised his eyebrows. "Some of her is ... as much as I could manage." He stared down at his creation with all the fondness of an indulgent father. "I've made quite a few refinements to the technology, mostly based on biological models. Her light source is living moss. Oxygen is supplied through a series of algae banks beneath the floor. As much as she can be, she is alive."

He watched the children as they walked around the pool, examining the sub from every angle. "I've been mapping changes in marine life for over twenty years," he said. "I needed Gaia to help with the work."

"But how did she end up here?" Beth was puzzled. She didn't know much about science, but it was obvious that Gaia was immensely valuable. Surely whoever supplied the money to build her hadn't intended for her to end up here, hidden in a hole in a rock beside North Berwick harbour?

"I ..." the professor caught himself, " that is, the university ... has a marine facility near Leith. That's where Gaia was built. But I needed someplace to hide her and this was the only place I could think of within reach."

Tom frowned. "But why did you need to hide her?"

"Gaia is a prototype," said the professor. "An experiment. Some things are not quite right yet."

"What things?" asked Tom, his voice suddenly suspicious.

The professor shrugged. His eyes drifted back to the submarine. "Oxygen conversion from the algae beds isn't quite perfect. And there's a little bit of a problem with the stabilisers when she surfaces. Nothing that can't be fixed." He looked back at the children and they saw his eyes moisten. "The project ran out of funding. They say she's too expensive to maintain or develop. They want to put her in a *museum*." He made the last word sound like a swear word.

"But she's not old enough for a museum," said Tom.

"Technology moves fast these days," sighed the professor. His jaw tightened. "But Gaia's not ready for the scrap heap yet. Not if I can help it."

"How could they?" Beth's voice was suddenly angry. "She's absolutely beautiful."

The professor nodded. "She is, isn't she? I couldn't let them do that. I waited till I was on my own and then ... I took her." He shook his head at the memory. "It was a terrible journey. She's not designed for a single person to operate. I barely made it." He laughed aloud, back to his usual bouncy self. "I imagine they've changed the security codes now that it's too late!"

"So that day at the demonstration, Gaia was already here?" Beth understood now why the huge crowds had horrified the professor.

"Yes," he said. "When I saw those two men, for

one awful moment, I thought they knew where she was. Had maybe even taken her already." His voice hardened. "It's not safe for her here. That's why I need you."

"Us?" Tom said. "But we're just kids."

"Nobody is *just* anything." The professor pulled what looked like a channel hopper from his pocket and pointed it at the submersible. Soundlessly, a hatch on the top slid open. "Would you care to step aboard?"

With a nimble little jump, he landed on a flattened area on the top, then slid down inside the hatch. He didn't disappear, though. Through the transparent walls, the children glimpsed his bulky shape moving around inside.

Tom looked at Beth. "No," he said.

"Oh yes," answered Beth, imitating the professor's leap on to the top of the sub. With a little wave to Tom, she slipped down inside. It was obvious that she wasn't coming out any time soon. With a mingled sense of anticipation and fear, he followed his sister's lead.

There was very little space to move around. Most of the interior was taken up by pieces of equipment, but everything was all very carefully and firmly stowed away.

"Algae beds," said the professor, pointing to a series of narrow channels filled with a gooey brown substance beneath their feet. "That's our oxygen supply."

Tom looked down at them dubiously, then let his eyes travel along a series of wires towards a narrow space at the back where a slightly larger version of the fuel cell they had seen before glowed with a soft golden light. But this one wasn't square. Everything inside the submersible followed the same shape.

"Curve city," said Beth, her face soft with wonder.

She was right, thought Tom. There were no straight edges anywhere.

The only thing that seemed out of place was the sleeping bag slung over the seat at the front of the sub. The professor saw Tom looking at it.

"I haven't been home lately," he said. "Too dangerous." He dumped the sleeping bag on the floor and squeezed himself into the chair. In front of him was a bank of dials and switches and a fan-shaped wheel.

"This is the control centre," said the professor.

The children looked around while the professor carried on talking, quickly rattling through things he had clearly said quite a few times before.

"Gaia is a one-atmosphere sub with an advanced life support system. No need to worry about depth pressure." He reached out and patted the hull. "The perspex body gives 360 degree visibility. Motive power and communications come from the fuel cell. Sometimes that has to be topped up."

He stopped abruptly when he noticed the blank look on their faces. "Sorry," he said. "Too much, too fast, wasn't it? I always get carried away. Any questions?"

Beth grabbed hold of the only phrase she could clearly remember. "What's motive power?"

"Ah," said the professor. "That's the energy she needs to come to life. She's built for a two man," he smiled at Beth, "... or woman ... crew. That's why I'm working on a voice for her. If she could understand and speak to me, then I wouldn't need any help. But right now, that's not possible."

Beth was eyeing the crank handle on the side of the fuel cell with deep suspicion.

"She needs a pilot, a navigator and someone to be in charge of life support." The professor's smile broadened as he pushed himself out of the chair and stood up. "With your help, I can take her somewhere safer, somewhere I can keep her until I work out what to do."

Tom took a deep breath. "Professor, we can't do this. Mum and Dad have no idea where we are and ..."

"It's completely safe," the professor brushed aside his objections. "Weather conditions are absolutely perfect. And you can talk to them just as soon as we get to open water." His smile broadened. "I have satellite!"

"But why us, Professor MacBlain?" insisted Tom. "We don't know anything about this sort of thing."

The professor's smile disappeared. "Because there's no one else," he said sadly. "Not even POP are willing to help."

"Tom," said Beth. "Gaia belongs here, in the sea. You don't want them to put her in a museum, do you?"

"No, of course not," said Tom. "But ..." He struggled to find a way out of the corner Beth and the professor had boxed him into, but he couldn't think of any argument or suggestion that might make a difference.

"It's perfectly safe, is it?" Tom still wasn't convinced.

"Here," said the professor eagerly. "Let me show you." He sat Tom down in a seat near the middle of the sub, at its widest part. "I need you to keep an eye on where we are ... this screen will show you. See that dot? That's us. The great big blob over here is the Bass Rock. We want to get close to catch the tidal race, but not too close. And this," he tapped a dial, "gives the depth reading. In metres."

"What's too close?" Beth was peeping over Tom's shoulder.

"Just let me know if you see us coming near any blobs at all, Tom. The screen is accurate to within ten metres ... and that's in real time too. Don't worry. I'll do the rest. Think of a clock face. Any obstacle has to be somewhere on the clock face. You just tell me what time it would be if the clock was pointing to it, right?"

"You mean like 'big blob at four o'clock'?"

"Exactly!"

The professor moved to the front and began rolling up his sleeping bag. He didn't seem to understand sarcasm, Tom thought, as he stared at the screen. And ten metres could make an awful lot of difference when there was a great big solid blob in your way.

"Beth," Tom said, trying to keep his voice low. "We can't do this."

"Why not?" Beth tore her eyes away from the screen and looked at him with a combination of hope and defiance. "It's safe. The professor said so."

"You know Mum and Dad wouldn't be happy about this, Beth. I'm not sure I'm happy about it either."

Tom flicked a glance at the professor, but he was totally absorbed in checking his equipment, tapping dials and twiddling knobs, humming softly to himself as he prepared for departure.

"But we'll never get a chance like this again," pleaded Beth. Don't you want to know what's out there? Aren't you curious? *Please,* Tom."

"We don't even know where we're going," said Tom.

This time, the professor did hear him. "Heading for Seacliff," he said cheerily. "Just a mile or so up the coast. Take us about an hour ... no more."

Beth's desperate eagerness and his own curiosity were too strong. Tom gave in. "All right. We'll do it."

To his surprise and embarrassment, Beth leaned over and gave him a quick peck on the cheek. "Thanks, Tom. You're the best brother ever!" Then she turned to the professor.

"What about me?"

Professor MacBlain came back to join them. "Your job, Beth, is to keep an eye on the life support system." He waved at the deep blue glow. "If the light starts to fade, then you need to let me know. I've got a supply of air cylinders in case of emergency. You need to watch energy levels too. That's here." He tapped the oval fuel cell that shone vivid yellow, like a tiny sun. "If the light dims, then turn this handle in the side."

"Why?"

"Because that means there's energy depletion," said the professor.

"No," Beth didn't understand what he meant, but she knew it wasn't an answer to her question. "I mean, why me? Again?" She pointed at the crank handle. "Why is it always me who has to fill the fuel cell?"

"Well," said the professor, "To be honest, it's really the best job Gaia has to offer. If energy remains constant, which it usually does, then you've got nothing to do except look at what's out there." He waved at the hull.

Beth considered for a moment, then she said. "Okay."

The professor beamed. "All ready then? Better strap in. Use the webbing harness on your chair, Tom. And Beth, you use the one above your head. That thing that looks like a cat's cradle." He took his seat, reached forward and stabbed a button on the console in front of him then took hold of the wheel.

The hatch above their heads slid shut. Tom stared at the screen in front of him, wondering how on earth he had allowed himself to be persuaded to join in this weird and wonderful adventure.

Smoothly and silently, Gaia slipped beneath the surface of the water.

Chapter 13

The engine came to life with a soft, deep rumble, almost as though Gaia was purring with delight at being once more on the move. The submarine turned slightly under the professor's guiding hand and they slipped into another tunnel, this one completely below the water line. Peering past the bulky figure of the professor, Tom saw a stream of light pierce the darkness. All around them, long streamers of mussels parted to let them through.

"I hope there's no iron around here," Tom said, remembering how the mussels had clamped themselves against the side of the tank at the professor's demonstration.

"Don't worry" said the professor. "There's no metal anywhere on Gaia."

All the same, a sudden thump against the wall of the sub sent the children's heads sharply round, convinced that the professor was wrong. Either that, or they had hit the side of the tunnel. Beth let out a gasp of horror when she saw something peering in at them, a purple monster with a flat, snout-like face and horrendous teeth.

The professor just laughed. "Don't worry, George won't bother you. He's just curious."

"George?"

"The wolf fish. He lives here. I know I shouldn't, but sometimes I bring him a little extra something to eat."

The engine rumbled on quietly as they slipped out of the tunnel and into a forest of waving fronds, not green, but a deep, dark red.

"Once we're through the kelp beds," said the professor, "You'll be able to see a lot more."

At first, though, the children had no time to look at anything. They kept their attention firmly fixed on their respective tasks, ready to leap into action as soon as any change occurred. When nothing happened to cause any alarm they gradually began to relax.

They emerged from the kelp forest, to find themselves gliding smoothly above a series of rocky gullies. Bright sunlight from above sent shafts of light slanting down through the clear water.

"Clear visibility today," said the professor. "Good for them up there as well as us."

The children looked up and saw they were passing beneath the hull of a small boat.

"Won't they notice?" asked Tom.

"No," said the professor. "Gaia is practically invisible from the surface when she's underwater." He waved an arm at the glowing walls. "All they can see when they look down is the deep blue sea."

Tom's eyes shifted back to the screen. He frowned in dismay. Surely they were going in the wrong direction. The hairs on the back of his neck prickled as he turned to Professor MacBlain.

The professor spoke without bothering to look up, almost as though he could read Tom's mind. "We'll be heading out past the Bass Rock to catch the tide. Saves energy that way. I did a lot of diving out there in my younger days." His voice softened. "I drifted this current many times. And now I'm doing it again with Gaia." His voice hardened. "Plus, there's something out there I need to check up on."

Tom and Beth exchanged a glance. It wasn't hard to guess what that something was.

The professor turned round and grinned at them. "Do you want to call your parents now?" He held out a pair of earphones.

"Let me do it," Beth stood up and slipped past Tom to take the earphones from the professor.

Tom didn't argue. Beth could bend the truth in any direction, like a piece of silly putty, without actually ever telling a lie.

Following the professor's instructions, Beth keyed in the number. "Hi Dad," she said after a minute. "Just checking in. We went for a walk … near the shore."

Tom raised his eyebrows and Beth made a face at him as she listened. "Yes … uhuh … yes. We should be back in a couple of hours. Yes, it is a lovely day, isn't it? We might have some chips, then head for the park."

Tom couldn't help but admire the way she made a whole string of vague remarks hang together, like a detailed plan for the day.

"Okay, Dad," said Beth. "See you later."

For the next twenty minutes or so, the children spent their time gazing quietly out at the world beyond Gaia's walls.

"It's weird," Beth whispered to Tom. "It feels like there's nothing between us and the water."

Tom nodded, his eyes following the path of a jellyfish as it slid past the side of the sub.

"When we're out beyond the rock," said the professor, "we'll start to move back in towards the shore."

Beth wasn't listening. She was watching a shoal of little fish flick past, followed by a pair of sleek, grey shapes. "Look at the seals!" She bounced up and down in excitement. "They're herding the fish like sheepdogs!"

Tom watched, equally unable to tear his eyes away, wishing he had Beth's job so he could spend more time staring through the clear walls at the world outside. His gaze flicked back to the dial and he jumped in alarm. "There's a big blob coming, professor! It's about ... erm ... eight o'clock!"

The professor nodded. "Right on schedule," he said. "We're just about at the Bass Rock. Get ready," he added, a tinge of excitement in his voice. "You're going to like this!"

"Can you give me depth reading, Tom?"

Tom checked the dial. "Fifteen metres, Professor."

"Right," the professor flicked a switch. "Engine off. No need to make Gaia work any harder than she has to. We'll let the tide carry us out to sea. Time to fly!"

The children watched, open-mouthed, as a huge slab of rock reared up alongside the sub. A sudden thump on the other side sent them whirling them around to see a whiskery face peering in at them for a moment before it slid away.

"A seal! Right outside the window!" Tom couldn't

believe it. He turned back to the other side. The professor was right to call it flying. They were speeding past an undersea cliff face, the light from above illuminating the life that clung to every nook and crannie.

The professor was calling out to them, words tumbling out of his mouth as he tried to explain what it was they were looking at.

"All those colours — the pink, red and yellow — those are anemones."

They slipped past a clump that looked remarkably like a bed of garden flowers, their fronds waving in the current. Beth couldn't resist waving back.

"You see those long white fuzzy things on the edge of that rock?" called out the professor. "That's digitatum. It's a coral. Most folk call it dead men's fingers."

"What's that?" Beth had spotted what looked like a tiny white hedgehog with bright yellow spines on top of the coral.

The professor peered through the side of the submarine. "Aha! You usually have to go a little deeper to see one of those. It's a nudibranch."

Beth smiled. It really was a pretty little creature. "What's it doing?"

"Feeding," said the professor. "They eat lots of different things. Including each other."

"Yuk!"

"It's a balance, Beth," said the professor with a hint of laughter in his voice. "A delicate balance. Every creature has a role to play"

"Look at those." Tom pointed to a ledge just ahead.

"Sunstars," said the professor. "A kind of starfish."

"I never knew they came in so many colours," muttered Tom, staring at the carpet of colour, scarlet and purple and orange.

The professor was clearly enjoying their excitement. He kept flicking his eyes towards them, a broad smile on his face. "Not so long ago, this river was dying," he said. "You couldn't even eat the mussels from Musselburgh. But lately, life has been coming back."

"Tom! Look!"

At Beth's shout, Tom turned to see a puffin swimming beside them with its head down, wings magically transformed into flippers.

Beth was grinning with delight. "Their feet match their beaks!"

It was true. They were orange at both ends. The puffin was a totally different shape underwater from how it was on the surface.

"It looks like it's flying." Tom grinned back at his sister. "Just like us!"

Another face peered out at them from a crack in the rock.

"Wolf fish!" the children exclaimed together, then gasped at the sight of another face peeping out at them from a wide cleft in the rock. Even behind the mask they could see the look of disbelief that passed across the diver's face as they flashed past.

The professor laughed. "He probably thinks we're a hallucination! He'll be checking his air supply and looking for his dive buddy now, I bet … to see if he saw it too! But Gaia's not so easy to identify! I'm taking her down a little further now," said the professor. "Give me a shout at thirty metres, Tom."

As they dropped further towards the sea floor, the light from above began to fade. Beth shivered a little, though the temperature inside the submarine hadn't changed and then let out a little gasp of surprise as she saw a golden ribbon of light emerge from the fuel cell, moving along the perspex beneath her feet until it reached the front. A moment later, the light reached out beyond Gaia to illuminate the undersea world.

As soon as Tom called out the depth, they stopped falling and began to move forward, round the side of the cliff. Beth shivered again as it grew gloomier still. Their smiles faded. Neither she nor Tom was looking at the sea life that clung to every rock. Instead, all their attention was focused on Gaia's other side, watching as the looming bulk of the tanker grew ever larger, until they were moving down a pitch black, narrow tunnel, with the tanker on one side and the cliff on the other. Above their heads they saw a jagged, barnacle-encrusted spur of rock. The golden light tilted upwards, illuminating what looked like thin streamers of pure darkness.

"Hmm ...," said the professor, his voice reassuringly matter-of-fact, "there's a bit of leakage, but only a very little. That's very good news."

To their relief, it was only moments later that the tanker slipped past and they were emerging on the other side, into the sea beyond the Bass Rock. Gaia's walls began to vibrate gently as the engines hummed back into life. The children suddenly remembered they had jobs to do and quickly checked to reassure themselves that all was well.

"That was the most wonderful thing I've ever seen," said Tom fervently when he had reassured himself that there were no worrying-looking blips on the screen. "Except ..." he bit his lip, thinking about the tanker and what it contained.

"It is wonderful," said the professor. "And fragile too. All it takes is one accident, one mistake ..."

"But it's safe down here, isn't it?" Beth waved an arm at the outside world. "Oil floats."

The professor shook his head. "Not for ever, Beth." He was peering ahead, obviously looking for something. "Eventually it sinks. And even before that, it cuts out the light from the surface. I started POP to try and get people to see the risks we're taking, allowing these huge tankers up the Forth, but mostly they just don't listen. They just tell me I'm mad."

"I don't think you're mad, Professor," Beth said softly.

"No," said Tom, gazing out of the window. "Not mad at all."

Professor MacBlain tilted the wheel and Gaia turned slightly to the left. "We're not finished yet. There's something else I'd like to show you. We should be passing over it just about ... now."

The engine quietened as Gaia slowed down. Tom and Beth peered down between the channels in the floor. Below them, an odd shape poked up from the seabed; a ragged spear point with something taller at one end.

"Is that the front of a ship?" Tom tilted his head from side to side, trying to bring the shape into focus.

"Yes," said the professor. "A German submarine from the Second World War. They called them U-boats. It must have been prowling around the mouth of the Firth. Probably laying mines. And then, someone found them."

"What about the people?" Beth stared down at the wreck. It was covered in the white coral the professor called dead men's fingers.

"I don't know," said the professor, his usually cheery voice flat and sombre. "I just hope they were rescued before it sank." His voice took on a slightly happier note. "But that was a very long time ago. And look at it now … it's full of life."

He was right. The wreck was covered in tiny fish, like little snakes, moving in and out of the gaps and holes in the boat's surface.

"Pipefish," said the professor. "There are more wrecks than you can count out here, and there are creatures living in all of them. So, you see, nature can recover from almost anything if it's given a chance. There's still hope for the future." He turned the wheel and they moved slowly away. "It's time to go. The tide's on the turn and we need to get Gaia to safety before the drag causes any problems."

Tom watched his screen carefully as the ship moved forward once again. "There's a really big blob directly ahead, Professor," he called out.

"That's because it's the mainland, you dummy," said Beth. She was confident enough now to spare the fuel cell only occasional glances.

They both turned to face the prow of the submarine and froze in horror at the sight of a great wall of rock looming up ahead. The professor seemed oblivious. He was muttering to himself, "Should be here somewhere, right about now ... ah, there we are."

Tom and Beth grabbed hold of each other in panic as Gaia surged forward into a gap between the rocks and then made a sharp left turn, sending the children swinging wildly to one side.

The professor cut the engine and turned to face them. "Made it!" he said cheerfully. "Welcome to Seacliff, the smallest harbour in Britain. Actually, there was no harbour at all until someone had the bright idea of blasting one out of the rock. Must have been quite an explosion!" He laughed. "People have been changing this coastline for a long time, but this is one change that definitely works in our favour."

He glanced at his watch. "And if I'm not mistaken, we should be just in time to catch the bus from Dunbar." He rubbed his hands together in satisfaction. "Nice work, everyone!"

Chapter 14

A snake-like tube dropped down in front of the professor, like an oxygen mask on an aeroplane. The children watched the rest of the tube uncoil outside the submarine and drift up to the surface. The professor peeked into the tube. "Nobody about," he announced. "Perfect!" Gaia rose to the surface, in a mass of bubbles, rocking from side to side.

Beth hung on to Tom, her stomach churning. "So this is what he meant by a little bit of trouble with the stabilisers."

The professor went up first, armed with a long pole with a brass hook at one end. He grinned down at the children. "Grappling hook," he said. "Makes me feel like a pirate!"

Once he had managed to draw Gaia close to the harbour wall he helped Beth up through the hatch. She struggled for balance as Gaia swung alarmingly to and fro, waiting for a chance to jump on to the slippery steps that led up the side of the harbour wall.

Back on solid ground at last, she staggered across to a handy rock and sat down, pale-faced and more than a little queasy. A moment later, Tom joined her, then the professor. He pointed his little gizmo at the sub and all three of them watched in silence as the hatch closed and Gaia sank quietly beneath the surface of the water.

They had arrived in a tiny harbour set in the middle of a massive rocky outcrop, but there was barely enough time to take in their surroundings before a woman and two little boys armed with fishing nets appeared from around a stack of lobster pots.

"Where did you come from? We never saw you on the beach," the older boy demanded. The smaller one peered at them from behind his fishing net, watching intently as if he expected them to disappear without warning.

The woman gave an embarrassed laugh. "Don't be rude, Rory," she said. But it was clear from the look in her eyes that she was wondering exactly the same thing.

"We arrived in a submarine," said the professor and laughed aloud when he saw the shock on Tom's face.

The professor winked at Tom as the two little boys peered into the depths of the harbour. Tom stepped forward and looked down with what he hoped would come across as nothing more than casual interest. He was relieved to discover that Gaia's transparent hull was impossible to spot unless you knew what you were looking for.

The woman hauled the two little boys back from the edge and ushered them away, declaring in a bright, artificial voice that all the best rock pools were back the way they had come.

"Where's the fisherman's boat?" asked Tom when they were alone once more. It was clear from all the ropes and lobster pots that someone used this harbour a lot.

"Getting a refit," said the professor. "Gaia should be safe here for a couple of weeks at least.

There's always plenty water in this harbour, even at low tide. And this little piece of equipment …" he waved the little black box in his hand, "will tell me if anyone tries to disturb her." He put the box in his pocket and rubbed his hands again. "I think it's time we were moving on."

The professor led the way along a narrow track between two huge red sandstone boulders. They emerged into the open to find themselves on the edge of a sandy bay.

"North Berwick is back that way," said the professor.

The children turned round to see a rocky shoreline. Foaming waves dashed against the foot of a sheer cliff. High above their heads loomed the towering bulk of a ruined castle.

"That's Tantallon," said Tom.

"I know that," snapped Beth, eying the steep climb with horror. There was no way she would be able to climb it.

"The way up is over there."

To her relief, the professor was pointing in the opposite direction, towards the wide expanse of beach. It was a sheltered spot, protected from the wind by a tree-lined hill, but unlike North Berwick, this beach was almost deserted. The woman and her two children had disappeared behind the rocks.

"Look!" The professor pointed to several black dots out on the water. "Surfers," he said. "This is one of their favourite places. It's very quiet. Not a lot of people come here. The track's too narrow and potholed for most people to risk their cars."

Behind the surfers was the massive bulk of the Bass Rock. "The rock looks absolutely huge from here," said Beth. "Much bigger than it looks from North Berwick."

"And so does the tanker," added the professor gloomily.

Tom was watching two figures in the water, paddling furiously into the rising swell. He saw their backs hunch, then they rose smoothly to their feet, riding the crest of a wave as it rolled steadily towards the shore, constantly bending and shifting their bodies to keep themselves just ahead of the point where the crest broke in a surging line of foam.

"That looks easy," said Tom. "But I bet it's not."

"How far is it to the bus?" Beth asked, as they scrambled down off the rocks and began to plod across the sand.

"Not far," said the professor. "Across the beach, up that hill, then another half-mile or so along the road."

Tom and Beth exchanged a meaningful look. The hill was almost as steep as the cliff below Tantallon, but they soon discovered that the track didn't go straight up. Instead, it meandered gently between the trees, leading them through a deep, green silence broken only by an occasional rustle in the undergrowth, or a brief snatch of birdsong.

The walk along the hard surface of the road proved much more wearisome and when the bus stop finally appeared in the distance, both Tom and Beth were so exhausted they had no energy left to talk. It wasn't long before the bus rolled up and they climbed gratefully aboard.

About ten minutes later, the bus left the fields behind and entered the outskirts of North Berwick.

"What are you going to do now, Professor?" The professor was in the seat just in front, but Tom kept his voice low. There were plenty other people on the bus.

"Don't worry, Tom," said the professor. "You've done your bit, and I am tremendously grateful. Everything will work out, you'll see."

"But how?" Beth turned from the window. "You said no one else would help you and you can't move Gaia on your own."

The professor smiled. "I may not need to. I've taken the university to court. They claim that until the case is settled she should remain with them. But they have no right to Gaia and I'm going to prove it. That's why they're so desperate to get her back, right now, before the case is settled." The professor wagged a finger and smiled his beaming smile. "But possession is nine-tenths of the law, as they say."

"So if they don't really have the right to take her back, why don't you go to the newspapers?" Tom was relieved to hear he hadn't really taken part in a theft. But the professor shook his head. His next words sent a chill down Tom's spine.

"I'm not allowed to publicise my work. Some of the funding was from…military sources. Not what I wanted, but I didn't really have a lot of choice."

"Anyway," said Beth decisively. "It doesn't really

matter where she ought to be, does it? What really matters is that nobody but us knows exactly where she is!" She grinned at the professor. "And we're not telling!"

The professor smiled back as Beth hauled herself wearily to her feet and pressed the bell. "We ought to get off here, Tom," she said.

Tom stayed where he was. "Why? This bus goes all the way down the hill to the harbour."

"Yes," she said. "But I don't think we should be seen with the professor."

"Good thinking, Beth," said Professor MacBlain. "You certainly can't." He leaned over the back of the seat and ceremonially shook each of them by the hand. "Thank you very much for your help. I couldn't have done it without you." He looked anxiously from one to the other. "You must promise me, though. You can't tell anyone about Gaia. Absolutely no one."

"Don't worry," said Beth. "We'll keep your secret. Won't we Tom?"

Her brother nodded, then stood up and followed her off the bus.

"You know that computer the professor showed us?" said Beth as they crossed the road and walked into the park.

"You mean the one he was teaching to talk?"

Beth nodded. "I don't think he should use his own voice."

"No," said Tom as they headed out of the gates and down towards the beach. "Gaia deserves a voice of her own."

Beth stopped walking and screwed up her eyes,

peering into the distance. "Is that Mum?"

It was. And Toby was with her, dashing in and out of the waves and then running in a wide circle round Mum before running back to the water again. When the children called out, he stopped, perked up his ears and rushed towards them, as though they had been away for months instead of hours.

Mum arrived in Toby's wake. "Hi there! Did you get your game of football?"

"No," said Tom. "But I had fun anyway."

"Well," said Mum. "You can tell me all about it when we get home."

"What are you doing here?" asked Beth.

"Your Dad sent me out. He said the fresh air would do me good. Especially with the builders arriving on Monday."

Beth smiled at her mother, thinking that dad had been right. The worry lines were gone from her face and she looked more relaxed than she had for ages. Best of all, she wasn't clutching that awful notebook.

Mum picked up Toby's ball and threw it back into the water. Toby scurried after it, oblivious to the angry cries of the sea birds resting on the sand.

"Gannets," said Mum, watching the birds circle above them. "Solan geese, they used to call them. They say witches used to leave their bodies on the shore and fly with the geese." She held up a hand to shade her eyes and looked across the water at the Bass. Her voice grew low, as if she was talking to herself. *"The bare and sea-girt Bass, with all its roaring multitude of waves."*

"What's that?" Tom was surprised. Mum wasn't the type to quote poetry, but that's what it sounded like.

"Just something from an old book," she said.

"How come you know so much about it?" asked Beth.

"I've been coming here a long time," said Mum, magically summoning Toby with a wave of her hand. "Dark history or not, I've always loved this place." She clipped the lead on to Toby's collar and stood up, taking a deep breath of sea air. "Come on then. Time to go home."

A delicious aroma drifted down the hall towards them when they came through the front door.

"I'll get the plates," Mum called from behind them as they walked down the hall and out the back door.

Dad had spent the afternoon tidying up the little back yard. He had cobbled together a barbecue from some discarded bricks and an instant charcoal kit. The children sat on a couple of kitchen chairs and watched as their father turned sausages and corn on the cob, making sure everything was browning nicely.

"The perfect end to a perfect day," said Beth with a sigh of contentment.

Dad smiled. "Looks like summer has arrived at last," he said. "And the house isn't so bad, is it? When there's no wind ... and no rain!"

Not even their cluttered bedroom seemed quite so bad when they climbed the stairs that night.

"You know what, Tom?" Beth's sleeping bag rustled as she turned towards him.

Tom grunted. He was almost asleep. He had brought the radio upstairs with him and was listening to a soft voice reading the shipping news. He hardly recognised any of the places mentioned, but somehow the slow, quiet voice giving details of wind and weather made this afternoon's adventure feel even more real.

"Those two men," said Beth, "must be working for the university. But we still don't know who that woman is, or why she's chasing the professor."

"I'm not sure that it matters," said Tom sleepily, as the voice from the radio droned on. "If she's after Gaia, then I think our job is to keep her as far away from the professor as possible."

Beth nodded and yawned, then turned over on her side. Soon, they were both asleep, dreaming of drifting with Gaia far out into the ocean, through an undersea world filled with brightness and beauty, where dead men's fingers reached out towards them through holes in the ocean floor.

Chapter 15

The next morning, the builders arrived bright and early, armed with hammers and crowbars. By the end of the day, they had almost demolished the kitchen, dumping everything they needed to get rid of in the huge skip that sat outside, causing problems for any vehicle heading for the harbour. A smaller group of workmen invaded the attic, eager to rip out the old broken window and demolish the wobbly walls. Everything that could be moved was squeezed into the room that smelt of apples and toast.

Tom and Beth spent the day outside with Toby.

"We must be getting fit, at least," puffed Tom, after a particularly wild chase across the beach ended with Toby back in the water.

"I think I've worked out how to get him back now. Watch this." Beth picked up a piece of waterlogged wood and threw it into the water. As soon as Toby saw it coming, he turned and swam towards it, grabbing it between his jaws, before turning back to the shore.

Toby dropped the stick at their feet and crouched low in front of it, his delight turning swiftly to dismay when Beth bent over and clipped the lead back on his collar.

"At least I've got something to do on Wednesday," said Beth. "Elsie says her Dad's got another boat trip going out. Isn't Connor coming back tomorrow? You can go back to playing football."

"I don't think so," said Tom. He didn't want to think about football. Not after last time.

"Well, you can always come with me," said Beth.

"Won't Elsie mind?"

"Not really." Beth picked up the stick, then turned to grin at Tom. "She says most of the girls in our class are bubbleheads, but some of the boys are all right."

On Wednesday morning, Tom inched his way cautiously past the fridge, brushed a coating of dust from a chair and sat down next to Beth, balancing a bowl of cornflakes on his knees. "I know you and Mum have to stay here," he said to his father. "But why us? We could have gone to stay with Grannie."

"Grannie's not home. She's away on a gardening tour." Dad's voice came from behind a pile of boxes. "She told me she was taking a helicopter trip to some island with a really big garden."

"Lucky Grannie," said Beth.

"What about the caravan?" Tom said. "Why can't we stay there?"

"It's already booked for the week," Dad said. "That's how Grannie paid for her holiday."

A rustle of newspaper announced Mum's presence in the space beside the window. "We're really sorry about this, kids," said Mum. "We didn't know there would be so much to do in the house. But it seemed like such a bargain ... we didn't think we could afford this much space with the money we had to spend." She sighed. "I might have known it was too good to be true!"

Tom and Beth glanced around and then exchanged a meaningful glance. But neither of them said anything. The room spoke for itself.

"I'm not sure we *can* afford this one." Dad stood up and added the builder's estimate to the pile of stuff on the table, then negotiated his way carefully across the room to the microwave and put his coffee cup inside to reheat.

Mum chose to ignore his remark. The newspaper rustled again as she turned a page. "Listen to this," she said after a moment. "It's about the tanker. Apparently there's over a million gallons of crude oil still on board. They're still trying to work out how to get it out the damaged hold. It says here they're prepared to mobilise for a major disaster if the weather changes."

Tom frowned, but Beth jumped to her feet.

"Are you coming Tom?" At his puzzled look she bent towards him. "If anybody knows what's going on," she said quietly, "It'll be the people at the harbour."

Tom quickly finished off the last few spoonfuls of his breakfast, wondering whether the gritty taste was too much sugar, or just a layer of dust.

Down at the harbour, Beth marched confidently up to a tall, lanky man with bleached blond hair. "Hi Danny."

The man looked down at them. The pirate costume was gone. Today he was dressed in shorts and a t-shirt. A smile of welcome appeared on his unshaven face.

"This is my brother, Tom," said Beth.

"Oh yeah." Danny tilted his head and looked

at Tom. "I saw you at the demonstration as well, didn't I?"

"Yes," said Tom. "But we left early."

"So you did," said Danny. "I hope you haven't brought that dog with you." His eyes crinkled up. He gave a deep laugh and slapped Tom heartily on the shoulder.

"Any news?" asked Beth eagerly.

Danny shrugged. "Tanker's still there, weather's still holding. Nothing new. We're still diving, but only off the Isle of May and Craigleith. Not the Bass Rock."

"But there are divers out there," Beth blurted, then clenched her teeth in pain as Tom's elbow caught her in the ribs.

"The news reports said they were out there inspecting the damage," said Tom quickly.

"That's right," said Danny. "It's my favourite dive site." His eyes grew dreamy. "It's truly amazing down there."

"The nudibranchs are pretty," said Beth. "But they're yucky really. They eat each other!"

Danny's eyes widened in surprise. "You've seen a nudibranch?"

This time Beth didn't need Tom to dig her in the ribs. She would have been happy to do it to herself. Twice in less than a minute she had let her mouth open without using her brain. She glanced at Tom, but he just glowered at her, unable to think of any way to get his sister out of the hole she had dug for herself.

"It was on one of those nature programmes on television," she said in sudden inspiration.

"But I thought you said you didn't have any electricity."

Beth spun round. She hadn't realized Elsie was standing right behind her. She thought fast. "I mean I saw it on the Internet. I did what you said ... I went to the library."

She spoke quickly. Too quickly. Elsie peered at her suspiciously from behind her fringe. Beth bit her lip.

"Oh yeah," Danny grinned his huge grin. "I've seen that clip. People diving off St Abb's Head. Cathedral Rock is really spectacular."

Someone called out Tom's name and Beth turned round, grateful for the distraction. Connor was jogging towards them. His face and his clothes were streaked with grass stains. He looked hot but happy.

"Hi Tom," he said as he came closer. "Thought I might see you in the park. The others were asking where you were. There were only five of us." He grinned. "Alex was on our team this time. We won. Seven nil!"

Tom smiled at Connor, who didn't seem to think that Tom had done anything particularly awful after all. "I could play tomorrow, if you like."

"Great," said Connor. Then his face turned serious. "Any news about the tanker?"

"I've been talking to that lot over there," Elsie nodded in the direction of the people clustered round the oil drum. "The divers are packing up. They've decided it's safe to pump out the rest of the oil. They'll be starting tomorrow."

"Good news at last!" said Danny. He turned

to look across the water where a cluster of little boats were busy round the huge bulk of the tanker. "Let's hope the weather holds. There's rain coming, but that shouldn't be a problem."

"You can tell just from looking at the sky?" Beth was impressed.

Danny laughed. "No," he said. "I listen to the weather forecast just like everybody else." He laid a hand on Elsie's shoulder. "Come on, then. Your mother wants to take you shopping after lunch."

Elsie groaned and Beth smiled in sympathy, although she wouldn't really have minded an afternoon raking through the shops with Mum, instead of watching her scribbling in that irritating notebook. Elsie didn't smile back.

They watched Elsie and her father head over to a mud-spattered old jeep and climb aboard, then Connor said, "I've got to go too. I promised Jacob we'd play snakes and ladders this afternoon." He made a face. "You know why they're called board games?"

"Because you play them on a board?" Tom knew that wasn't going to be the answer, but now that football seemed back on the agenda, he was happy to let Connor lead him in whatever direction he chose.

"Wrong." Connor shook his head. "It's because they're really, really boring."

Tom laughed. He waved goodbye to Connor then turned to his sister.

"Come on, Beth. We'd better go and fetch Toby. He's been stuck in the back yard all morning." He gave her a thoughtful look. "I almost thought you'd lost it there for a moment, you know. But I think you managed to scrape your way out of it."

Beth just shrugged. She felt really uncomfortable about lying to Elsie. Somehow, over the last week or so, the other girl had turned into a proper friend instead of just someone to hang around with. Now she probably wouldn't want to be friends any more. The thought was surprisingly painful. Beth wanted to run over to the jeep and explain everything, but that wasn't possible. Not just because Elsie's dad was there. It was because she had a secret that wasn't hers to tell.

"Hebrides, Bailey, Faroe. Wind north-easterly. Weather rough, becoming rougher. Warning of severe gales to follow."

Tom yawned as the radio voice droned on, comforted by the knowledge that the bad weather report was for the far north. Outside, rain fell in steady sheets. Every so often, a car swished past outside. Inside, there was nothing but the sound of Beth's steady breathing. She had been unusually quiet all evening, until Mum sent her to bed early with a hot water bottle. Tom rolled over and let the sound of water gurgling down the drainpipes lull him to sleep.

It felt like only moments later that he opened his eyes to find the pearly sheen of an overcast dawn lightening the sky. Something tugged at his consiousness, but at first he couldn't work out what it was.

"Beth!" he said. "Are you asleep?"

"What do you want?"

Chapter 16

As Beth climbed out of her sleeping bag and pad-
ded across the room, they heard the mournful
sound of the foghorn sending its warning up and
down the coast. She peered through the window
and saw curling tendrils of mist drifting across the
rooftops. "Well, there's no wind now."

"We need to get down to the harbour," said Tom,
unzipping his bag and reaching for his clothes. "I
want to know what's been happening."

Beth shrank from the thought of facing Elsie's
cool grey eyes. But Tom was right. The people at
the harbour would know what was going on. "I
suppose we'd better get down there then," she said
without enthusiasm.

"Come back and let me know what's going on,"
called Mum as they squeezed their way towards
the front door past piles of equipment dumped by
the builders.

Beth nodded. "Sorry, Toby," she said as a hope-
ful face peered round the corner of the kitchen
door. "Not this time."

Someone had lit a fire in the oil drum and a
huddle of grim-faced people crowded round it
listening to the radio, damp and miserable from
the mist and rain. It was a local station, but the
radio announcer sounded calm and matter-of-fact,
as though she was reporting something taking
place a long way away. "High winds are predicted

for the Firth of Forth. The crippled tanker, *Nora Gallow*, is now at serious risk of further damage. Emergency services are on standby. We'll bring you further news as it comes in."

A woman in a hooded raincoat turned round and Beth blinked in surprise. It was their teacher, Mrs Ferguson.

"The storm was heading out over the North Sea," she said to the children. "But the wind changed direction. Now it's coming straight down the river. And when the tide turns, the wind and water will be driving the waves in the same direction. There's going to be some massive breakers out there."

"But the wind's died down." Tom was desperate for some good news.

Mrs Ferguson fixed him with a very teacherish look. "Have you never heard of the eye of the storm?"

Tom was saved from having to answer by the arrival of a large van. A woman opened the driver's door and jumped down on to the pavement, then moved round to the back doors. As she opened the back of the truck and began pulling out piles of equipment on to the ground — spades, ropes, plastic overalls, goggles and lots of other things the children didn't recognise — people down near the harbour dropped what they were doing and hurried towards her.

"What's going on?" Tom asked.

"We've all got jobs to do," said Mrs Ferguson pulling on a hat and gloves. "We always hope something like this won't happen, but that doesn't mean we're not ready for it if it does." She bent to pick up a backpack and shrugged it on to her shoulder. "That van's brought the equipment we need. We're off to Seacliff. If there's a spill at the Bass Rock, then that's where we need to be. It's the closest point."

"Seacliff!" Beth exchanged a surprised look with her brother, then her eyes travelled past Tom and she felt herself shrink a little inside as she saw a battered old jeep draw up behind the van. Beth couldn't bear misunderstandings. They made her feel uncomfortable, as though her clothes were a size too small. And she couldn't think of any way to fix this one.

"Let's go home," she said. "We promised to tell Mum what was happening."

"All right," said Tom. "But we'll be back."

As they left the group beside the oil drum, a slight breeze tickled their faces, then danced across the road ahead of them, scattering the fog.

"Look!" Beth grabbed Tom's arm as they were walking towards the house.

Squashed into the little space between the skip and the front door was a familiar, tubby figure. He seemed to be arguing with whoever was inside.

"We should let him know about the people heading for Seacliff," said Beth.

As they came closer, they heard his voice rise until he was almost shouting. "You don't understand! I have to speak to them!"

Dad was standing in the doorway, his normally cheerful face set in stiff lines. When he saw Tom and Beth, his frown deepened even further. He turned back to the professor. "Whatever you have to say to my children, I'm sure you can say it in front of me."

The professor blinked at him. Then he turned and stared at Tom and Beth as though he had never seen them before. "Children," he said thoughtfully.

"The professor seems very anxious to talk to you." Dad shot them a 'what have you been up to' kind of look, then turned his attention back to Professor MacBlain.

The professor squared his shoulders and took a deep breath, "You're right," he said. "They are children. And I'm very sorry to have bothered you." Then he turned and walked quickly away.

All three of them watched the professor as he hurried up the street. "Dad," said Tom urgently. "Can't we just have a quick word with him?"

Dad thought hard for a minute, then winced as a volley of bangs and thumps came from inside the house, followed by a resounding crash.

"All right," he said at last. "But don't be long. I'm not having you hanging around with peculiar strangers."

By the time they caught up with him, the professor was in the car park. He was fussing with a tarpaulin that covered the back of a small green truck, working his way round the edges, carefully tucking in the sides.

Beth tapped him on the shoulder. "What's wrong, Professor?"

He turned round and the children saw his face, more serious than they had ever seen it before. He made a pathetic attempt at a smile. "Nothing's wrong, Beth. I just wanted a word with you. It wasn't important."

"Are they still after you and Gaia?" asked Tom. "Those men from the university and that other woman?"

The professor's face crumpled. "None of that matters any more."

"It's the tanker, isn't it?" said Beth.

The professor nodded. "If that ship comes off the rock, it will be a disaster. I have to get to Gaia."

Beth remembered what they had to tell him. "We wanted to warn you. Loads of people are heading for Seacliff."

"I thought they might," the professor said grimly. He tied one final knot and tugged at the tarpaulin. There was a strong whiff of the sea. "I came to ask for your help again," he said, turning to the children. "But I wasn't thinking straight. You've already done more than enough. Both of you. Your father is right. It's far too dangerous." He looked earnestly into their faces. "I want you to know, you were the best crew I ever sailed with."

Tom opened his mouth to argue then closed it again as a sleek black car drew up beside them. With hurried movements the professor finished tucking in the tarpaulin. Nobody was surprised when the doors opened and the men in suits climbed out.

Tall Suit didn't spare the children a glance. "We meet at last, Professor MacBlain, You're a hard man to track down."

"I have nothing to say to you," said Professor MacBlain. "You can tell your employers I'll see them in court." He began to walk round the side of the truck to the driver's seat. Short Suit stepped in front of him.

"There's no need to go to court, Professor," he said. "It's an expensive and very public process that does none of us any good. Without the university, you would never have got the funding for your submarine. And all research results are the property of the university. You know that as well as I do."

The professor bristled. "Right at this moment," he said, "ownership is the last thing on my mind. If you'll excuse me, I'm a very busy man."

With an agility that surprised them all, he jumped into the truck, started the engine and sped off up the road. The men in suits exchanged a look.

"He can run, but he can't hide," said Tall Suit, in a mock Hollywood accent.

Short Suit laughed. Then he looked at the children. "I was right," he said. "I knew if we kept an eye on you two we'd find him ... and his stolen submarine."

"Her name is Gaia!" Beth was suddenly furious with these men, who seemed to care about nothing except getting their property back. She stabbed a finger in the direction of the water. "Don't you care about what's happening out there?" She was shouting now.

Tall Suit looked down at the children. "Sorry kids," he said, "that's not our business. Our job is to do what we've been paid to do. We can't afford any distractions."

"Let's not waste any more time." Short Suit opened the car door. "He's heading east. Next harbour is Dunbar. That's the only place with a big enough boatyard for the sub ... oops ... I mean Gaia." His eyes gleamed in amusement as he nodded to the children and climbed into the car.

The children stared after them for a moment, then Tom bent down and picked something off the ground. It was a mussel, glistening wet, still with the briny smell of the sea. He stared down at it, remembering that sudden explosion of movement when the mussels had whacked against the side of the fish tank in the basement at Jubilee Hall. Things were coming together inside his head.

"He *is* mad," whispered Tom. "Absolutely barking."

"What do you mean?" Beth let her eyes leave the distant shape of the car heading up the hill and turned back to her brother.

"Remember the green glue, Beth?"

She nodded.

"Remember what the mussels need to make their glue?"

"Iron!" Beth eyes flashed with sudden understanding. "It's iron, isn't it? And that's what the tanker is made of." She looked at the mussel in Tom's hand. "He said those ones were specially bred. They make a huge amount of glue."

It was Tom's turn to nod. "If he can get the mussels to the tanker, then they can stop a leak. As long as they have something to fix on to."

The children turned together and looked back towards the harbour, where the distant shape of

Chapter 17

"Tom?" Beth's voice was urgent. "We have to help him!"

"You know," Tom said thoughtfully, "If we don't like where we are, we can move somewhere else."

"So?" Beth didn't know what he was talking about and she didn't care.

"But that's not possible for George, is it?"

"George? … Who's George?"

"The wolf fish, remember?" Tom said. "George has to stay where he is, even if everything he eats is covered in oil … even if it means he gets covered in oil as well. And what about the seals? And the puffins. And all those plants and animals under the sea? George doesn't have a choice. None of them do."

"There's always a choice," said Beth firmly. "For us at least."

"I don't think so," said Tom. "I'm me and you're you. It doesn't matter how much you think about it … you'll always end up doing the same thing. And the same goes for me. Look at those two." He nodded in the direction of the disappearing car. "They were never going to help, were they?"

Beth felt a hot anger bubble up inside her. It looked as though once again Tom's ultra-cautious approach to life was going to get in the way. And this time, it would be disastrous. "Well, I know what my choice is," she snapped. "What's yours?"

Tom drew back his fist and hurled the mussel after the disappearing car. "The same as yours, of course. The professor may be mad, Beth, but he's the only one who's going to try and do something about it! We have to help him. We can't just hang around here while all that life out there is choked to death!"

"I know," said Beth, all anger gone. They stared at each other for a long moment, each one seeing their own dread and determination mirrored in the other's eyes.

"We have to get to Seacliff," said Beth. "And we can't get there on our own. Not in time to catch up with the professor. We'll have to try and get a lift from someone."

Tom looked up at the sky. The mist was gone. A gathering of darker cloud suggested that the rain would soon get much heavier. "We'd better get a move on. We'll pick up our jackets on the way."

Neither of them said anything as they hurried home, their minds too full of fear for that fragile, magical world deep beneath the waves, a world that was perilously close to disappearing forever.

When they squeezed past the skip and opened the door, they found the house strangely silent.

"The builders must be having a tea break," said Beth.

"Sorry kids," Mum appeared in the living room doorway. "The electricity's off again. Shouldn't be long, though. What's happening with the tanker?"

Tom and Beth's news brought a worried frown to her forehead. Beth grabbed her jacket from its hook. "We need to go back to the harbour. They're all there waiting for news."

"Okay," said Mum. "It's getting cold out there though. Maybe you can go to the cafe and get yourselves some hot soup." She headed back into the kitchen. "I'll get my purse."

She reappeared a moment later with Toby weaving round her feet, getting in the way as usual. She sighed. "I don't suppose you could take him with you?"

"We can't take him into the café," Beth said quickly.

"And we can't take him with us to the harbour," added Tom. "He's just a menace around other people."

"Odd," said his mother. "I never seem to have any trouble with him at all."

Seized by a sudden impulse, Beth threw her arms around her mother and hugged her tightly. "I love you, Mum."

"I love you too, Beth," said her mother, hugging her back. She let go and looked at her daughter curiously. "What brought that on?"

"Nothing," said Beth as she tugged the front door open. "I just felt like it." She stepped quickly out the door, hoping her mother hadn't heard the sudden hoarseness in her voice.

At that moment, the sound of hammering started up again and Tom took advantage of the distraction to follow his sister out the door. "We'll see you later, Mum. Don't worry. Everything's fine."

Outside, the wind was picking up. Blinking their eyes to clear them of the dust and grit swirling up from the skip, they quickened their pace. Mrs Ferguson had been right. The rest of the storm was still to come.

When they reached the harbour, it looked as though they might be too late. The van was gone and the group round the oil drum had disappeared.

But Danny's jeep was still there, with Elsie beside it, pulling on a pair of waterproof trousers. Tom and Beth hurried over to join her.

"Where's everybody gone?"

"Seacliff," said Elsie abruptly. "The way the tide's going, that'll be where the oil is likely to hit the shore." She finished with the trousers and lifted a parka from the back seat of the jeep.

Beth glanced over at the harbour. The Greenpeace boat was on its way out, people scurrying around the deck, doing complicated things with ropes and pulleys. She nudged her brother and raised her eyebrows. He took the hint and wandered over to the deserted oil drum. Someone had poured water on it to make sure it was out.

"Elsie," Beth said, "I have to talk to you."

"What about?" Elsie stuck her head inside the parka without waiting for Beth to answer.

"I know you thought I was telling a pack of lies yesterday," said Beth, uncomfortably aware of all the times in the past she had twisted the truth to suit herself. But not this time. She took a deep breath. "Well ... you were right. I was."

"I don't care if you tell me lies." Elsie's voice was still muffled by the parka but Beth could tell there wasn't much warmth in it.

"But I care!"

Elsie's face popped out of the top of the parka and Beth stared into her eyes, willing her to listen.

"I can't tell you why I lied," she said. "I promised someone I wouldn't tell. But there's something I have to do and I can't do it without your help."

"Is this something to do with Professor MacBlain?"

Beth stared at her in surprise. "What makes you say that?"

Elsie shrugged. "I just guessed. Connor said you went to his demonstration. Then I saw you talking to him at the protest meeting. And besides," she added with a slight smile, "I saw him standing on your doorstep when we were coming down the road."

"You may think the professor's crazy," said Beth eagerly, "but he's got an idea that might protect the river if the tanker gets holed. Without me and Tom to help him, I don't think he can make it work. He's already at Seacliff, Elsie. We have to catch him before he ..." Beth stopped. She'd lost control of her tongue once before. She wasn't going to let it happen again.

Elsie stared at her for a long moment, then glanced across at Tom, who was sifting idly through the soggy mass at the bottom of the oil drum with a charred stick.

"You're right," Elsie said at last. "I do think the professor's weird. But he's also an expert on marine life. Including nudibranchs," she said with another sharp glance at Beth. "If anyone can do something to help, it's him." She thought a moment longer, then finally made up her mind. "Wait here. I'll have to ask my dad."

Beth waved at Tom. He dropped the stick and walked back to join her. "I think it's going to be okay," she said. "As long as her dad agrees to take us."

Already anxious to be gone, they watched Elsie disappear inside her father's shop. It felt like an endless wait before she came out again, bringing Danny along with her, but it was probably no more than a couple of minutes. Danny was carrying a couple of boxes and Elsie's arms were wrapped round what looked like a tent bag. The children waited impatiently as he fitted everything into the back of the jeep and crossed the road to join them.

"You want to go to Seacliff?" he asked.

Beth nodded. "We want to help."

Danny scratched his stubbly chin and thought for a moment. "Well, if you think you can be useful then you're welcome to join us. But not without your parents' permission."

Tom already had his phone out. "Would you speak to them, then?" He dialled the number and held it out.

They listened to one side of a typical extra polite conversation between two grown-ups who didn't know each other. Elsie's dad explained where they were going, and how long they were likely to be, then handed back the phone so that Tom's mother could tell him to stay out of the rain and be sure to say please and thank you.

"I'll drop you back at your house in a couple of hours," said Danny. "I guess we'll know by then, one way or another. Where do you live?"

"It's just down the street." Beth pointed. "The one with the skip outside."

"Oh, that's you, is it?" Danny didn't seem too pleased.

"It'll be gone in a couple of days," said Beth, hoping he wouldn't change his mind now that he knew they were the criminals who were blocking the road.

"Okay then." Danny gestured towards the jeep. "Let's go."

Chapter 18

Beth and Elsie climbed into the back seats, leaving Tom to sit in the front with Danny. There was no chance for them to talk privately in the crowded jeep, so they sat in silence, listening to the sound of the windscreen wipers and the whoosh of tyres rushing through puddles as they sped out of North Berwick and along the coast road towards Seacliff.

Danny seemed oblivious to the white line down the middle of the road. The children found themselves holding their breath as they careered towards each bend, only letting it out again when they rounded the corner to find the road clear ahead.

Finally, Beth leaned over and whispered in Elsie's ear. "Does he always drive like this?"

"This is nothing," said Elsie. "Just wait till we get to the track down the hill,"

Within a few minutes, the jeep was passing the bus stop and taking the turn off for the beach. It took almost no time at all to cover the distance that had taken so long when they walked it with Professor MacBlain.

As they reached the top of the potholed track, Beth tapped her brother on the shoulder and pointed out of the window. He was just in time to glimpse the back end of a small green truck tucked away behind a hawthorn hedge.

Tom nodded his head, but didn't speak. All his

attention was suddenly focused on keeping himself upright as they bumped and slid their way down the potholed road to the car park at the bottom. Last time they had been here, the car park had been virtually empty, but today it was nearly full. The were several other mud-spattered jeeps, including one belonging to the coastguard and another from the rangers service, plus the van they had last seen at the harbour, its rear end now gaping open and empty.

"I see they've brought an argocat," said Danny, eyeing up an odd-looking vehicle with six huge tyres on either side. "That'll be handy for the beach. Right, you lot … out you get."

He hauled the tent out the back of the jeep and led the way down to the beach. After seeing what had come out of the van, Tom and Beth half expected to see the beach covered in plastic-suited figures, their faces masked and anonymous. But so far everyone was still dressed in their ordinary clothes. Above their heads, the clatter of first one, and then another helicopter passing overhead told them that the coastguard were also keeping a close eye on events out at sea.

Danny stopped and looked around. "I have to find the Beach Master. He's in charge of all this. I need to find out if he wants me to fetch the cages."

"Cages?" Beth asked.

"For the birds," said Danny. "If there's a spill, this is where they'll start to come ashore."

"But there could be hundreds of them!" said Beth. There didn't seem to be enough people around to deal with that many.

"Not hundreds." Danny's face creased in a worried frown as he began to walk across the sand. "Thousands. And there's no way we can save them all. Most of the local divers are trained in animal rescue. I've helped out with injured seals ... and a porpoise once. But never anything like this."

He pointed to a sheltered spot in the lee of the hill where people were busy setting up various pieces of equipment. "I don't know how long we'll be here. Set the tent up over there, next to Frances. She's keeping in touch with Greenpeace on the radio. Don't wander off when you're finished," he said, his normal good humour deserting him. "The weather's not getting any better and I've got other things to worry about than having to chase kids around the beach." He dropped the bundle at their feet and left them to it.

"Who's Frances?" Tom turned enquiringly to Elsie.

"Connor's mum," she said.

Tom turned back in surprise to see Connor plodding towards them across the sand. He grinned at Tom and Beth. "What are you two doing here?"

"It's a long story," said Tom, as he heaved the tent into his arms.

Beth tugged at his arm. "We're running out of time," she said urgently.

"I know," Tom's voice was tight with frustration. "But it's not going to be easy."

He was right. There were people everywhere. And Danny had made it very clear that they couldn't just leave without permission.

To their enormous relief, the tent was the type that simply snapped open. On Elsie's instructions, Beth hurried off and found a couple of rocks. She tossed them inside the tent to stop it blowing away.

"Tom," she said. "We need to go. Now."

"But you're supposed to stay here with us." Connor looked from one of them to the other, puzzled.

"We can't," said Beth. "We have to go. Right now."

"She's right," said Tom. "We have to get to the harbour."

Elsie was chewing her lip, thinking hard. A sudden gust of wind whipped her fringe off her face to reveal a pair of very dark brown eyes, and a jagged red scar just below her hairline. She saw them looking.

"I had an accident on the dive boat," she said.

Beth smiled at her. "I think you look just like Harry Potter."

Elsie allowed herself a small smile back. "That's why I don't go out on the boat so much any more." Then she turned and yelled, "Dad!"

"Can we go up the hill?" she asked when her father walked over to join them, "I thought I'd take these two up to the haunted house."

Tom and Beth exchanged a look of surprise and relief. Elsie was going to help them after all.

Danny frowned. "This isn't a day out at the seaside, Elsie."

I know that, Dad," she said, "but I really don't think I can bear to watch."

She meant it too, Beth realized. It wasn't just an excuse.

Danny looked at Elsie for a long moment. Then he shrugged. "Fair enough," he said. "At least you'll be out of the wind."

"I'll come too," offered Connor. "It's better than standing around waiting for a disaster to happen."

"Let's go then," said Elsie. "Once we're near the top you can get round to the harbour without anyone seeing you."

"I wish someone would tell me what's going on," grumbled Connor as all four of them headed towards the hill.

"I'm sorry, Connor," said Tom. "It's just too complicated. And we made a promise."

Beth climbed steadily up the hill beside Elsie. Danny was right. Up here, the wind died away almost to nothing. It wasn't particularly wet either. Most of the rain was caught by the spreading leaves of the trees and bushes and what did get through swiftly disappeared beneath the surface of the sandy soil.

"Thanks, Elsie," said Beth. "I hope you won't get into trouble."

"Don't thank me," said Elsie. "I don't know if I'm doing the right thing or not. All I know is, nobody knows these waters better than Angus MacBlain. If he has a plan, then I'm sure it's worth a try."

"How long have you known him?" asked Beth,

"All my life," said Elsie. "He's always lived here. He used to dive with my dad."

"The professor doesn't look like a diver." Beth smiled at the thought of that tubby shape in a rubber suit and duck feet.

"Actually, he's a very good diver," said Elsie, "but he hasn't done much lately. Not since he began his big project with Waverley University." She gave Beth a sharp look. "He called it the Gaia project."

Beth couldn't prevent the look of surprise on her face. Elsie stopped walking and said, "Is that what this is about? The Gaia Project?"

"Sort of," mumbled Beth. Then it occurred to her that if Elsie was asking the questions, then maybe she could tell her a little bit more without breaking her promise to the professor. "What do you know about it?"

"Not much." Elsie started climbing again. "But I know it was something big. There was a POP meeting a few weeks ago ... not the one you tried to get into. This one was private. Grown-ups only. There was a big argument."

"I could hear them arguing from upstairs," said Connor's voice behind them. "There was a lot of shouting and door-slamming ... mostly the professor, I think. Then he set up his stuff in the basement. But after that he just sort of ... disappeared."

"Do you remember those men in suits?" Tom thought that was safe at least. "They're from the university. He was trying to keep away from them. And that woman."

"What woman?"

"The one in the red bobble hat," puffed Beth, grabbing hold of a tuft of grass and hauling herself up the hill.

"Oh yes," said Elsie, who didn't seem to have any trouble climbing the hill and talking at the same time. "He's definitely trying to keep out of her way."

Beth would have asked more, but Connor tapped her shoulder and pointed through the tangle of thorny bushes and stunted trees. Beth stared at the huge house on the summit of the hill, her eyes travelling across the ivy-shrouded walls, dotted with blind, gaping windows and its tall, pointed turrets. It looked like something straight out of a horror movie.

"You should see it when it's getting dark," said Connor, "When the moonlight shines through those windows ..." He raised his head and let out a spooky howl.

"It's not really haunted, though," said Elsie. "We just like to pretend it is."

"Seacliff's a funny place," said Connor. "The people who lived here were wreckers. They used lights to make the ships think there was a safe harbour here. And when they ended up on the rocks..." He let his voice die away suggestively, then looked up at Tom and Beth, his eyes wide. "There's even a cave over there where they found an ancient altar and lots of human bones. Oh yes," he said in a dramatic whisper. "There are a lot of secrets around here."

And now there's another one, thought Tom. He glanced up at the shell of the house. At any other time, it would have been irresistible, but not today. Instead, he followed Elsie as she threaded her way up over a pile of fallen branches and stopped at a small sandy hole in the side of the hill.

All four turned automatically to look at the view. If Elsie had hoped to escape the sight of the tanker, thought Beth, then she was going to be disappointed. Their high vantage point gave them a clear view of the Bass Rock.

"The tide must be on the turn," said Connor. "Look at those waves."

The children watched as the wind and the tide between them built a swelling surge of water that rushed down the estuary towards the rock and broke there, sending huge columns of white spray shooting up into the air.

Elsie sat down on the ground and looked up at Tom and Beth. "I'm not going to ask you any more," she said, "except for one thing. Are you doing something dangerous?"

Beth wasn't going to lie again. "Yes," she said, "but we don't have any choice. The professor has a plan. Without us, he won't be able to do it."

Elsie stared at her for a long moment. Then she pointed to a narrow trail leading into the bushes. "If you follow that, you'll end up at the side of the cliff. There's a track leading down to the shore. It comes out just beside the harbour." She turned to Connor. "We'll stay here, and make sure dad sees us from time to time."

"Thanks, Elsie," said Beth, feeling uncomfortable all over again. She hadn't lied, but she hadn't mentioned that the professor didn't know they were coming. "We'll be as quick as we can."

"Right," they heard Connor say as they set off along the track. "Now will you tell me what's going on?"

Chapter 19

The track across the hill was easy to follow, although their desperate sense of urgency made the journey feel much longer than it really was. Even so, there were places where they had to go down on their hands and knees to crawl beneath tall bushes armed with needle sharp thorns.

"It's a good job our clothes are dark," said Tom when they emerged from the cover of the bushes at a spot where the side of the hill had fallen away, leaving nothing but an empty sand hill. Anyone looking up from below would have seen them immediately.

Beth nodded her agreement. She scurried quickly across, casting a nervous glance back towards the camp, but none of the figures hurrying around the nest of tents seemed to be aware of them. They had other things to think about.

After only a few minutes, they came up against the rocky wall of the cliff face and stopped to look around. It was clear from the flattened grass and the broken branches littering the side of the path that someone had been down this path just a little while before them.

The damage to the bushes extended all the way up the side of the cliff. Tom looked down and saw that the trail carried on across the sand and shingle in a long, wavering line, as though some enormous snake had recently passed this way, weaving its serpentine way towards the sea.

"That's either the Loch Ness Monster's brother," said Tom, "Or Professor MacBlain with a net full of mussels."

"He must have dragged it all the way from the truck," said Beth. "I can't believe he managed it on his own."

One behind the other, they followed the trail downhill until they reached a sand dune covered in sharp-bladed sea grass. The rain was much heavier now, driving a stinging combination of salt and sand into their faces. Above their heads, the cliff top ledges reverberated with the noise of angry seagulls objecting to their presence.

The wind had whipped up the waves. Huge breakers were smashing into the rocks with a thunderous crash, sending spray shooting high into the air. And for the first time, they could see the tiny square that was Seacliff Harbour. There was a brief moment of horrified silence before Beth grabbed hold of her brother and pointed across the rocks towards the harbour.

"Tom, we're too late! He's leaving!"

They watched in horror as a flurry of bubbles rose up from the bottom of the harbour. Dimly visible, a shape beneath the water began to turn towards the gap in the harbour wall. No longer caring whether anyone saw him or not, Tom slipped and slid his way down the sand dune with Beth in close pursuit.

They raced across the shingle and on to the slippery rocks, leaping recklessly from one boulder to another until they reached the narrow, foam-flecked stones of the harbour exit.

"Professor!"

In the water below them, they saw the figure behind the transparent hull raise its head. Tom and Beth jumped up and down, waving their arms, yelling as loud as they could. Slowly, Gaia came to the surface, blue light winking from deep inside. She was still as beautiful as they remembered, but there was no time now to admire her.

They saw the professor move back down the sub towards the hatch. "Go home!" he shouted, when his head finally appeared in the open air. "This is no place for you!"

Tom and Beth slid their way round the slippery stones towards him. "No!" yelled Beth. "We're not leaving!"

"You have to let us come with you, Professor," said Tom, kneeling down on the stone and leaning out over the water.

He shook his head. "I can't. This could be very dangerous."

"Not half as dangerous as that tanker is for everything that lives out there," said Beth, pointing out beyond the foaming surf towards the Bass Rock. "And you know you can't do it by yourself." She saw the professor hesitate and pressed home their advantage. "You know we're right, Professor."

The professor pressed his lips together and shook his head. "No," he said firmly. "I'm not taking you with me."

"At least you can let us help with those." Tom pointed to the huge net like a giant string bag, lying beside the harbour wall. It was full of mussels They had been wrong. The professor wasn't quite ready to leave yet.

Without giving him time to argue, Tom walked over to the net and picked up the thick rope attached to the end of the net. "What do you want me to do with this?"

The professor sighed. "All right then," he said. "You can help me with the mussels."

He clambered up out of the hatch, keeping his balance with difficulty as Gaia twisted from side to side, slopping water inside the hatch.

"I'm going to pull them along behind me, so we need to get them into the water. But first I need to attach the rope. Gaia has a towing bar on her rear end."

"I bet that's uncomfortable," said Beth.

Tom giggled. It came out a little more hysterically than he meant it to. He sobered up as another thought popped into his head. Did the professor actually mean to come up alongside the tanker and then go outside the submarine to untie the knot? Tom shivered. That was more than just dangerous. It was suicidal.

Professor MacBlain was silent for a long moment. Then he said, "There's a smaller rope that keeps the net closed. It fixes on just above the towing bar. The release mechanism inside Gaia lets me open the net. If I release the mussels at the right moment, then the tide should carry them towards the spur of rock and the tanker. The steel hull should set them off. I'm hoping there will be enough of them to seal the gap between the tanker and the rock and keep the tanker where it is."

Tom guessed that the professor had just fought — and won — the temptation to let him go on thinking the worst. It might have helped to change their minds about going with him. But it would also have left them thinking that he wasn't coming back.

The professor disappeared for a moment, then reappeared with his grappling hook. He used it to bring Gaia round so that the back of the submarine was right beside the wall. When he jumped ashore, Tom passed him the end of the rope and watched the professor tie it neatly and professionally to what looked like a small, looped fin at the back of the submarine.

He gave it a couple of sharp tugs to reassure himself, then stepped back on to the submarine and turned to the children. "I'll take her out a little. You two slide the rope into the water a bit at a time ... I don't want any knots. Give me a wave when you've only got a few feet left."

He disappeared below and they heard the thrum of the engine as Gaia moved away from the harbour wall. The ropes were heavy and hard to manage, especially the big one, but they struggled as best they could with its greasy unyielding weight, letting it out bit by bit.

When almost all of it had slithered into the water, they gave the signal and the professor brought Gaia back towards the wall.

"Right," he said as he re-emerged from the hatch, "Let's get the net in the water."

He joined them on the narrow quayside. Together they pushed and tugged and heaved, dragging the net full of mussels across the stones, until at last it toppled over the edge into the water.

"I don't know how you got that thing down the hill on your own," said Tom, filled with admiration for the effort it must have taken.

"It wasn't easy," the professor said grimly. "And I'm grateful for your help getting it in the water, but now I have to go."

"We're coming too." Beth planted herself right in front of him, her hands on her hips. "It's not up to you, Professor," she declared. "It's up to us. It's our choice. We're here because we're prepared to take the same risks as you … if there's a chance of saving all that life out there."

Tom gazed at Beth in admiration. She had a talent for argument. That was something he had always known, sometimes to his cost. But this time, it was Beth at her very best. There was no sign now of the timid sister who had been so nervous when she faced the men in suits in the basement of Jubilee Hall.

The professor glared at her. "I can risk myself," he said, "but I will not risk the lives of two children."

Beth glared back, her eyes flashing. "That's our future out there, Professor MacBlain. You know you can't get Gaia where you need to go without at least one other person. And there's nobody else to help you. Except for us. Without us, you might as well not bother."

The professor stared back at Beth while the wind sent his wild grey hair whipping about his hat and dashed spray into his face. At last he said, "It won't be like last time."

"We know that, Professor," said Tom earnestly. "We're not doing this for fun. We're doing it because we have to."

The children stared at him, willing him to agree. But in the end he shook his head.

"I'm sorry," he said. "I can't do it."

"Fine," said Beth. "Then you don't leave us any choice."

She turned away from him and took a flying leap on to Gaia, slipped down the hatch and inside. Without giving himself time to think, Tom took a jump and followed her lead, leaving the professor standing beside the hatch with his mouth open.

Chapter 20

"I still think this is a very bad idea," muttered the professor as he watched the children strap themselves in. He took off his hat and scratched his head. "I'm not even sure how it happened."

Beth turned to look at him. "Do you want to waste any more time arguing?" She didn't sound triumphant, just determined.

"No" said the professor. He lifted his hat and settled it firmly on top of his wild hair. "There's no time left for that."

He moved forward to look over Tom's shoulder at the sonar screen. "You remember that?" He pressed his finger on a dot of light. "That's the Bass Rock. Let me know if it splits into two lights instead of one."

Tom knew what that would mean. He stared at the lights, almost afraid even to blink in case it changed position.

The professor stabbed at another light. "That's the Greenpeace ship, I expect. But they can't do anything except watch. Although we might get some help from them in an emergency."

Tom swallowed. It should have been comforting to think that the ship was out there, but he didn't see how it could be much use if they were underwater and the ship was on the surface in a raging storm. He didn't ask what kind of emergency the professor might have in mind. He didn't want to know.

The professor moved past him to talk to Beth. "We should be all right for air, but if not, there's a couple of tanks stowed over here, in the space right at the back." He tapped the energy cell. "This is what you need to keep an eye on. It's going to take a lot more energy than usual to haul all that weight behind us."

Beth stared at the bright yellow light in the fuel cell. It looked healthy enough to her, but then she didn't really know what a fuel cell might look like when it was running out of energy.

"How will I know there's a problem?" she asked, her voice wavering slightly.

"You'll know," said the professor, turning away and moving up the submarine. "The light will start to dim."

Tom looked over at his sister as the professor moved up the submarine to take his place. He lowered his voice to a whisper. "Are you scared, Beth?"

"Of course I'm scared!" She snapped. The tension was making her jumpy. She took a deep breath to calm herself down. "Sorry," she said. "The sooner we get this over and done with, the better."

"All right then," said the professor. Above them, the hatch slid silently shut. "Time to go."

They slipped smoothly beneath the water and a moment later were negotiating the sharp turn out of the harbour, beginning a slow progress down the narrow channel leading from the harbour to the sea. The depth of the channel gave some protection from the violence of the waves above them, but the water that surged up the gap from the sea to foam and bubble around her sides, left Gaia struggling to make headway, until their progress was reduced to little more than a crawl.

"We'll be moving against the tide," said the professor. "It's not something I would normally choose to do, but there's nothing we can do about it." He leaned forward and adjusted a couple of switches.

The constant pressure forcing them backwards did have one advantage, as they discovered when Gaia jerked to a sudden halt, sending them swinging wildly about inside.

Beth peered at the view beyond the back wall of the submarine. "It's the net," she announced. "I think it's stuck."

It seemed as though their journey was over before it had even begun.

With a muffled curse, the professor unbuckled his harness. "I'll have to get up there and fix it."

But just then, another surge of water swept past them and they felt Gaia leap forward.

"It's come free." The professor sat back in his seat and took the wheel again. The next time it happened, he simply waited for the next wave to release them. Soon the stone walls of the channel gave way to barnacle-encrusted rock and shortly after that, the rock walls disappeared from sight. They had reached open water.

Tom and Beth peered through the hull, but it was impossible to see any distance in any direction through the murky grey water. There were no landmarks, nothing to tell up from down and only a blip on the screen to show what might be lurking only a short distance away.

"Sorry about this," said the professor, as Gaia lurched from side to side. "There's quite a swell on the surface and we're sideways on to the tide. We'll steady up when we reach deeper water."

"This is what you call a swell?" Beth spoke through gritted teeth. "I'd hate to be out in a storm, then."

Both children jumped in fright as something long and dark slapped against the front of the sub. It clung for a moment before it began a long, slow, slide all the way along the side of the submarine until it finally let go and disappeared behind them.

"Don't worry," called the professor. "It's just kelp. It's been torn loose from its moorings." He turned his head towards them. "You won't be able to see much of anything, I'm afraid. The swell is stirring up sediment from the bottom. That's why I need you to keep a careful eye on the screen, Tom."

As Tom hurriedly turned his eyes back to the screen, the professor leaned forward and pressed one of the buttons on the console. He turned a dial and suddenly the air was full of clicks and whistles. This was followed by a deep, single note a little like the sound of the foghorn.

Beth looked up in surprise. "What's that?"

"I'm sending a message." The professor's voice was grim. "There could be whales and dolphins in the area. I'm telling them to get out of here. Now."

Tom swallowed. Gaia was still rocking and his stomach was doing flip-flops. He glanced at Beth and she made a face back at him.

After a minute or two, the professor pressed a button and the noise stopped. "Water's deep enough now. Just going to adjust direction slightly."

The children sighed in relief as the submarine turned a little to the left and began to move more smoothly.

"Okay, that's good." The professor glanced over his shoulder. "You should have the rock on the starboard side ... I mean on the right," he corrected himself. "North Berwick will be on the left ... that's the port side. Let me know if we get too close to the shore."

"What's too close?" Tom snapped out the question. The professor seemed to have forgotten that he wasn't a trained navigator, but a very nervous boy.

"Just make sure there's about an equal distance between the rock and the harbour. That way we know we're heading down the middle. And there's nothing else out there. Not for a wee while anyway." The professor's voice was reassuringly calm.

"Why are we going up the river?" Beth turned round from her pointless peering through the gloom. "We're getting further away from the rock, not closer."

"The stabilisers won't cope if we try to make our way straight across," said the professor. "We'd probably end up just spinning out of control."

Tom and Beth shuddered at the idea. The slight rocking before they turned with the tide had been bad enough.

"We'll take a course round the back of Craigleith Island," the professor went on. "We can turn there without fighting the flow too much. Tom, let me know as soon as you see something coming in at the top of the screen." The professor turned round to look at them, his face grim.

"Once we're moving with the tide, things should get easier, but the first half of this journey is going to be hard work."

"Silly me," muttered Beth. "It was the second half *I* was worrying about."

Chapter 21

Their journey against the tide was far slower than the last time they had been out with the professor. The engine noise was different, more high-pitched, as though Gaia were whining with the effort.

"Is the engine supposed to sound like that, Professor?" Beth asked, in a voice high with tension.

"She's toiling, poor girl," said the professor. "It's not just that we're travelling against the tide. We've got a lot to haul." He reached out and patted the wall of the sub. "Not much further now, Gaia." He turned to look at Beth. "I think it would be a good idea to lend her some of your energy now, Beth."

Beth nodded. She took hold of the crank and began turning it without complaint. This time it wasn't a matter of fairness. It was a matter of survival. *At least it gives me something to do,* she thought, her eyes fixed on the fuel cell, wondering if she was imagining it, or whether the yellow light really was a little dimmer than it had been when they set out.

Gaia struggled on, a tiny blue and grey speck in the vastness of the undersea world. Strange objects tumbled past them in the gloom, too dark and twisty to be identifiable. Beth jumped as something clunked against the hull.

"It's worse now … the swell," she said.

Tom nodded. "If it's like this down here, it must be terrible on the surface."

They fell silent, both thinking of the storm that raged above them and the crippled tanker being battered by wind and waves, but gradually, despite their worries, the children found themselves lulled into an almost hypnotic calm, until suddenly Tom was jerked into awareness by the appearance of another blip on the screen.

"Craigleith Island up ahead, Professor. I think."

"Thanks, Tom."

They tilted in their seats as the professor began to turn Gaia to one side. Once again they were swinging from side to side in the turbulent water. Tom heard Beth groan in dismay, but he didn't look round. His eyes were fixed on the screen, watching as Gaia shifted position, moving slowly forward until the island lay to their right instead of dead ahead.

"You can take a break now Beth."

Gratefully, she sank back into her seat as the submarine steadied once again, moving behind the island and back into the tidal flow. This time, though, they were heading in the opposite direction and Gaia had no need to struggle to make headway. She was rushing along with the tide towards the open sea.

From what Tom could see on the screen, the professor was steering a course that would barely avoid a collision with the Bass Rock. It was exactly what he had expected, but all the same he felt a tightness in his chest and had to force himself to breathe more slowly. "Bass Rock dead ahead, Professor."

"Right. Keep your eyes glued to the screen. Let me know when we're fifty metres away."

"How far is that on the screen, Professor?" Tom struggled to keep the panic out of his voice but Beth heard it. She turned to look at him.

The professor grunted in annoyance, but not at Tom. "Sorry. Two squares of the grid."

Tom held his breath, watching. "That's ... now!"

"Time to start work again, Beth," said the professor. He flicked a switch and a beam of golden light cut through the darkness outside.

"Professor! The rock!" Beth yelled, as the undersea cliff loomed out of the murk.

"I see it."

Tom was no longer watching the screen. There was no point. Rigid with tension, he saw the thin golden line slide across the face of the cliff until at last it picked out the spur of rock that jutted out into the dark water. With her free hand, Beth reached out and took Tom's hand in hers. Clinging on to each other for comfort, they braced themselves for the worst.

"Come on, Gaia," pleaded the professor, as they moved with frightening speed towards the canyon-like space between the rock and the hull of the tanker.

But this was a canyon with one moving wall. The tanker was no longer firmly attached to the rock. It hadn't yet broken free, but it would soon. They didn't need the black spirals of oil seeping from the damaged hold to tell them that the waves were shifting the tanker to and fro from one moment to the next. Worst of all, the movement was cutting off the space they needed to move through to reach the safety of open water.

"I'm opening the net ... now!"

But just as he reached out a finger to stab one of the buttons on the console, there was a massive explosion of sound, a hollow, echoing boom that reverberated through the water, filling their heads until there was no room for conscious thought. The tanker had finally broken away from the rock.

There was a moment of total silence, then Beth whimpered, "We're not dead!"

The silence was followed by a grinding, crunching noise and Gaia jerked suddenly to a halt, throwing the professor forward. His head hit the console with a resounding crack. Beyond the walls of the sub, they saw the murky water darkening even further as swirls of inky blackness spread all around them.

They watched in terror as the professor slid sideways and crumpled on the floor.

"Professor!" they yelled. He didn't move or respond.

"He must have forgotten to fasten his harness," said Beth in a horrified whisper.

Tom didn't answer. It was impossible to hear her voice in the clanging, reverberating cacophony that resonated all around them. Both children snapped themselves free and rushed forward to where the professor hung sideways in his seat, his head lolling.

"It's the net!" Beth had to scream to be heard above the sounds from outside. "We got rid of the mussels ... but the net's stuck!" She shook the professor hard, but he only groaned.

Tom risked a look behind them. Beth was right. The gap behind them had disappeared. There was no space left between the tanker and the rock. He glanced ahead and his heart lurched in his chest. The front of the tanker was also moving closer to the cliff. There was almost no time left before they were flattened against the rock like an ant beneath a shoe.

Fighting to keep his balance as the sub rocked back and forwards, Tom eyed the control panel. There were buttons and lights. Lots of lights.

"Do something!" Yelled Beth. "Anything! Hit them all if you have to!"

Tom reached out and pressed a button close to where he thought the professor's finger had hovered. The dolphin noise filled the air.

"That's the wrong one!" screamed Beth.

Tom took a deep breath and raised both hands, ready to hit every single button, when Gaia shot forward with a suddenness that sent them both flying backwards. With tremendous relief, they realized that the horrendous noise was fading into the murky darkness behind them.

"The net must have torn free," said Tom, grabbing hold of the back of the professor's chair and hauling himself upright. He put his head in his hands, unable to believe that they were still alive.

Beth was kneeling beside the professor, shaking him hard. "Come on," she yelled. "Wake up!" She shoved her fist in her mouth, trying to keep herself from screaming. If they couldn't wake him up, they would be left tumbling forever in this empty wasteland.

Or perhaps not forever. One of her hands slid sideways and came away sticky. For one horrified moment, she thought it was blood, but she soon realized her mistake. Her hand was covered in brown goo. She looked down and saw a crack in the covering that sealed the algae in place. She had no idea how much of it was escaping, but she knew that without it, Gaia would soon run out of air. Her heart sinking, she looked up. They were still tumbling forward, still heading for the vast emptiness of the North Sea.

She watched in horror as the oxygen-bearing algae oozed slowly across the floor.

Chapter 22

"What ...? Where ...?" The professor looked vaguely up at Beth. "Ah..." he said in a conversational tone. "Now I see where Einstein went wrong..."

Beth shook him, hard. "Professor! Come on! You have to wake up now!" She gave him one last shake just to make sure and whimpered in relief when she saw awareness finally dawn on his face.

His eyes focused on her. Then he looked around. "I was just about to open the net ... wasn't I?"

Beth shook her head, not an easy thing to do when Gaia was throwing her from one side to the other. "You did open it, but there wasn't enough room between the tanker and the rock. Gaia got through, but the net was caught, just like at the harbour." She shuddered.

"Professor," said Tom, his voice urgent. "We don't know where we are."

The children struggled to keep their balance as the professor hauled himself back into his seat. He turned back to the control panel.

"That was close," he said in a small voice. "Too close. But there's no time to worry about that now." He began pressing switches and peering at dials while Tom and Beth made their unsteady way back to their positions.

"Tom ... get me a fix on the mainland. We'll have to be quick. The tide is determined to pull us out to sea."

Faint creaks and groans behind them told them the tanker was still settling against the rock.

"I think the water's getting clearer," Beth said with a note of hope in her voice.

Tom thought she might be right. The dark swirls of oil were slowly clearing, although that didn't necessarily mean they had done what they set out to do. It could just be that they were moving further away from the source. But he kept his mouth shut and said nothing. They had enough to deal with without worrying about things they could do nothing about.

Beth fixed herself back in her seat, pale but determined, and looked down at the fuel cell. She had been right. It definitely wasn't as bright as it had been. But that wasn't the worst thing.

"Professor," she said. "The algae stuff is leaking."

The professor glanced round and saw the thin grey ooze flowing across the bottom of the submarine. "We're going to have to hurry," he said. "We don't want to run out of air."

It was far too soon, he knew, but as soon as the professor said it, Tom felt his throat closing. Somehow it already felt harder to draw air into his lungs. He struggled hard to get his fear under control and focus on providing the information the professor needed to get them out of here.

From the high-pitched note coming from the engine, it was obvious that Gaia was struggling desperately to move sideways against the current. For endless minutes, no one spoke a word, until at last Professor MacBlain gave a small sigh of satisfaction. Gaia's engine was no longer screaming with the strain, though it was still a long way from the smooth contented purr the children remembered from their last trip.

"That's the best I can do," said the professor, taking off his hat to wipe his forehead. "We're on course for the shoreline, and Gaia is working hard to keep us going. Beth, I think we'll break out the air tanks now."

Beth fumbled around with the cylinders, while the professor gave them brief instructions on what to do if they needed to use them. After that, Tom and Beth swapped places, giving Beth a break from cranking power into the fuel cell while she took his place at the navigation screen.

The extra activity soon had him hot and bothered, wondering how much extra air he was using to keep the fuel cell powered up. "Can't we go up?" he asked, after taking a moment to use the cylinder.

The professor shook his head. "We can't surface yet. Not in this weather. Not with the stabilisers the way they are. We'd just end up tumbling around in the water. All we can do is head for the shore and hope we get there before Gaia runs out of energy."

His voice faded away and silence fell again, broken only by the sound of Gaia's laboured effort to get them safely back to shore.

After what seemed like an eternity, Beth called out, "Land ahead, Professor ... about two squares away on the grid."

"That's the good news," said the professor grimly. "The bad news is, we've got no chance of getting back into the harbour now the tide has turned. Gaia hasn't got enough power left to fight her way up the channel."

"Then what are we going to do?" Tom exchanged a fearful look with his sister, remembering that sheer rock face broken only by the small gap that led to the safety of the harbour.

"Ah well," said the professor. "There is one way to the shore. Its all a matter of who — or what — you are."

"What are you talking about?" Beth snapped. She wasn't in the mood for puzzles.

"Tantallon Castle is there for a reason," said the professor. "It's safe from attack by sea because no boat can find a safe harbour below it." He turned round and grinned at them. "But that doesn't mean that we can't. Because we are not a ship."

The children stared at him. This was definitely not the moment for a history lesson.

"There's no break in the rocks," he went on, "But there is a stretch of open water just beyond them."

"But how can we get there?" Tom frowned. It seemed like the professor just wasn't making any sense.

"We're going to surf, my friends." The professor gave a hoot of laughter as he turned back to the console. "Prepare yourselves for the ride of a lifetime!"

"He's mad," said Tom. "He really is mad."

"Well," said Beth. "It looks like this is our only

chance, Tom, so let's hope madness works."

The professor busied himself once more with his dials and switches. Gaia howled with the strain as the engine fought to keep her steady in the water.

"What are you waiting for?" shouted Beth.

"Every seventh wave, my dear," said the professor. "That's the big one!"

"I wish he'd just get on with it," muttered Tom through gritted teeth. It was getting harder and harder to breathe and he was afraid to let go of the crank handle to take advantage of the oxygen cylinder beside him. If Gaia's engine ran out of energy, then there was no hope at all.

"Here we go!" yelled the professor. "It's now or never!"

Tom's scream wasn't fear. He had gone beyond that. It was a howl of sheer excitement as Gaia rose higher and higher, riding the crest of a massive breaker that took her above the rocks to land with a crashing, bouncing thump in the shallow water beyond.

The professor let out a shaky laugh. "Promise not to try that at home." He pressed a switch and the hatch slid back. Tom opened his mouth wide, gulping in great lungfuls of fresh air.

The children clambered out, hampered by the fact that Gaia lay tilted to one side among the scattered boulders at the foot of the cliff. Deafened by the roar of the waves that rushed towards the rocks and broke in a surging tide of foam, they slipped and slid their way across the rocks, clinging on to each other as they staggered towards the safety of the beach.

There was no way of knowing if their effort to prevent a spill had been a success. They were both simply grateful that the professor had done such a good job of bringing them back to land. Tom tapped Beth on the shoulder and pointed. The beach was only a short distance away. Beth nodded and bent her head against the wind, forcing her wobbly legs forward until at last the slippery rock gave way to shingle and then soft, smooth sand.

They stopped and looked out to sea, waiting for the professor to catch up. Despite the wind and rain, they could easily see the Bass Rock. But still it wasn't its usual shape. The back end of the tanker was sticking out from behind the rock like a great tail. Two helicopters hovered in the air above it, and a whole flotilla of boats encircled it.

"I suppose that's the coastguard," said Tom.

"And Greenpeace as well," said Beth.

The professor arrived beside them. "Well," he said, following their example and looking out to sea, "We did our best."

"Yes," said Beth. "We made a good team, didn't we?"

"The very best, said the professor with a grin. Then his eyes travelled past the children and the smile froze on his face.

They turned around.

"Oh no," said Tom.

Silently, the three of them watched a familiar figure plod purposefully towards them. When she got close enough, she jammed her bobble hat more firmly on her head, folded her arms and stood there, waiting.

Chapter 23

Suddenly, everything was just too much. "Why can't you leave him alone?" Beth yelled. "You should be giving him a medal, not chasing after him! If it wasn't for the professor ..." she stopped, horrified to realize she had almost given away his secret.

The woman stepped back in surprise and the professor laid a hand on Beth's arm.

"It's all right, Beth," he said wearily. "Kirsty doesn't mean any harm. She's just worried about me, that's all." He looked over at the woman. "Well it looks like you finally caught up with me, doesn't it?"

The woman gave an exasperated snort. "I've been trying to catch up with you for ages, you silly old fool. But it's not what you think. I wanted to tell you I was sorry, Angus. You were right. Gaia should be here ... and so should you. POP needs you both."

"But what about the others?" The professor's eyes had lit up with sudden hope. "Last time I talked to them, they said I should let the university keep her."

"We've talked about it a lot since then," she said. "I've been arguing your case every chance I got. And now I've got most of POP behind me on this. We'll fight the university together. And there's a good chance we'll win. Especially if we get the press on our side."

The professor gave a gleeful laugh and rubbed his hands together. "I knew you could do it, Kirsty!"

"And what are you two doing here?" the woman turned to Tom and Beth, giving them a long, measuring look. But there was a twinkle in her eye.

"We came to help the professor," said Tom. "Nobody else was going to."

Beth was staring at the woman, a sudden suspicion blossoming in her mind. That small, round body, the grey, flyaway hair beneath that red bobble hat. She looked just like the professor. She glanced from one to the other, suddenly sure she was right.

"You're twins!"

The woman — Kirsty — nodded. "Yes we are. And he's always been a bit of a trial."

"I know what you mean," said Tom, with a sideways look at Beth.

Kirsty laughed. "The family call him Mad Angus," she said. "Except for me. I just call him Angus. Because sometimes he's right ... mad or not." She looked across the water at the tanker, then turned back to her brother. "Exactly what have you been up to this time?"

The professor shrugged. "Just saving the planet, Kirsty. Well, the Firth of Forth, at least." He stepped forward and grabbed her sleeve. "I need you to take care of the children. I have to get back and check on Gaia."

But Kirsty shook her head firmly. "No way, Angus. She's safe enough for now."

Angus cast a long look behind him, then looked back at Kirsty pleadingly. She shook her head again.

"If she's not in the harbour, then I suppose you came in over the rocks." She held up a hand as he opened his mouth. "No, please don't give me any details. I don't think I could cope. But if she is under the cliff, then no one can see her. Especially with all this going on."

She waved an arm towards the tanker. One of the helicopters had dropped a rope, lowering something — or someone — on to the deck.

"Is there any news yet, Kirsty?"

Kirsty shaded her eyes to look out across the water. "We've still got radio contact with Greenpeace, but it's all been a bit confusing. They say there's no doubt the *Nora Gallow* came off the rock, but there's hardly any sign of a leak so far. They're wondering now if maybe she somehow slid back and sealed the hole again, but that would be quite a miracle."

Angus smiled but Kirsty's eyes, when she looked back at her brother, were as hard as pebbles. "I don't know what you were thinking of Angus, taking these children out there with you."

"It wasn't his fault," said Beth. "He told us not to come, but we wouldn't let him go on his own."

"Well," said Kirsty. "At least he got you back in one piece, more or less." She peered at her brother more closely. "What happened to your head?"

The professor's hand went up to his forehead, fingering the swelling bump with an air of surprise. "I'm not really sure. It's a bit hard to remember. Did you mean it, Kirsty? About Gaia?"

Kirsty nodded. "If Gaia stays here, we can keep an eye on what's going on under the water. And she'd be useful too if we get any whales or dolphins lost upriver." She smiled. "POP is going to launch a publicity campaign. We'll do everything we can to make sure she stays here with you."

The professor let out a whoop of excitement and jumped forward to give his sister a bear-like hug. Kirsty laughed and pushed him away.

"First things first. Let's get these two back where they belong." She turned to Tom and Beth. "Your parents are here. They decided this was more important than a few wobbly walls. But there's no need to worry," she added as she saw the look of horror on both their faces. "They don't know you went missing. Although they are wondering why you're so keen to play hide and seek on the hill with Connor and Elsie with all that's happening out there. They brought the dog as well. He seems much better behaved when he's with them." She laughed as she turned away. "Come on then. Let's go."

The wind was still high, sending the waves surging into the tidal pools, leaving behind clouds of white sea foam, but the rain had stopped and clearer skies in the distance suggested that the storm would soon be over. Even before they reached the camp, they could see people buzzing about like a nest of disturbed ants.

"One thing, Kirsty," the professor said to his sister as he headed for sheltered corner, "I just can't work out how you always seemed to know where I was."

"Ah well, Angus," Kirsty tapped her finger against her nose, "You're not the only one who knows how to use technology." She reached into her pocket and pulled out a small object, like a chunky compass.

The professor was still puzzled. "But where's the transmitter? I've been moving around all over the place."

"In your hat, Angus!"

Kirsty beamed as the professor put his hand up to his head to discover his hat was no longer where it should be. "I've left it with Gaia!" he said, half-turning as though he meant to go back and fetch it.

"Leave it be," said Kirsty firmly. "I'm sure Gaia will look after it for you."

As they arrived at the huddle of tents, Connor and Elsie hurried down from the hill to join them.

"What happened?" Elsie cast a doubtful look at the professor's face, her eyes lingering on his bruised forehead.

"We did our best," said Beth. "But I don't know if it made any difference."

"You can tell us all about it later," said Connor firmly. "Right now you look like you could do with some hot chocolate."

Beth leaned over and spoke quietly in Tom's ear. "Do you think the mussels have done the job?"

"I hope so," said Tom. "But we can't be sure. Not yet."

Gratefully, the professor and the children allowed themselves to be led between the tents towards a small fire burning in a circle of stones. They sank down beside it and gratefully accepted a mug apiece. The hot chocolate tasted heavenly, but they didn't get more than a sip before a small furry shape suddenly leaped between them, almost into the fire, then began barking and chasing his tail.

"So you finally got here!"

They looked up to see Mum standing above them. She raised an eyebrow.

"I don't know why you were so desperate to come," she said. "You've been so busy playing with your friends that you've missed all the excitement."

Chapter 24

"Has anyone seen the paper?"

The children looked up briefly as Dad came into the room and then bent their heads back to the newspaper spread out on the table in front of them.

"What's up?" Dad poked his head between theirs. "You're not usually this interested in the news."

"It's about the tanker, Dad," said Tom.

"Listen," Beth began to read the article out loud.

"A tanker has glued itself to the Bass Rock ... with the help of the humble mussel. Thousands of people have been holding their breath over the last few days, waiting for news of the crippled tanker, the Nora Gallow. *Rescue services have been standing by up and down the coast, ready to spring into action in an attempt to save the coastline from a massive environmental disaster."*

She paused for breath and then read on, almost squeaking with delight. *"But now it seems that when stormy weather threatened to pull the tanker off the Bass Rock, the local mussels baffled experts by creating vast quantities of the glue-like substance they use to anchor themselves in the water, creating an impenetrable barrier between the rock and the ship."* She looked up and grinned at her father.

Dad smiled back. "Looks like the world out there knows how to take care of itself, then," he said.

"With a little bit of help from some friends," said Beth, her smile growing even wider.

Tom laughed and Dad looked from one to the other, his face puzzled. Beth quickly lowered her head to the paper and began to read again.

"As for the bird life, they're probably pleased. It's pretty crowded on the Bass Rock and the tanker will no doubt soon be converted to nesting space."

"I don't know about that," said Dad. "I imagine they'll get the tanker free pretty soon."

Tom laughed. "I wouldn't be so sure of that, Dad. Those mussels are pretty good at hanging on."

The door opened again and Mum came in. Beth and Tom groaned when they saw the notebook in her hand. Dad groaned too, but more quietly.

"Don't worry," she said. "I've got news. Some good, some bad."

They all sat up and tried to look interested.

"Right," said Mum, winding her way between the household equipment to find a place to sit. "The first piece of news is good from my point of view, but bad from yours. I've got a job. In the Tourist Information Office. I start next week."

"Do you have to bring your own mop?" asked Beth. Tom sniggered and Mum glared at them.

"Try to be sensible about this, would you? It means we are staying here. Permanently."

The children opened their mouths to speak but Mum held up a hand. "I haven't finished yet." She waved the notebook in the air. "I've been talking to the builders. It's quite clear that we can't stay here while the work is being done, so that means you two will be going back to town for the summer.

You can stay with Grannie now she's back from her big adventure. Dad and I will stay in the caravan, so we can keep an eye on things here."

"No way!" Both children yelled at the same time.

"We can stay in Grannie's caravan with you," said Beth. "There's plenty of room. After all, we're not going to be indoors very much at all."

Tom jumped to his feet and zipped open his fleece to reveal the t-shirt underneath. "I've joined the SAS," he said. "The youth section. Connor's doing it too."

"Don't be silly, Tom," Dad gave a nervous laugh. "The army doesn't take kids." He glanced nervously at Mum. "They don't, do they?"

"It's not the army, Dad!" Tom pulled off the fleece and turned round to reveal the message on the back of his shirt … "Surfers Against Spills."

"Ah," the relief in Dad's voice was obvious. Beth giggled.

"And I'm joining the diving club," she said. "Elsie's dad says I can next year, when I'm twelve. And in the meantime, he'll let me help out so I can save up for the equipment."

Mum smiled. "See? I told you this was a good place to live if you'd just give it a chance!"

Beth pulled a crumpled leaflet from her pocket and handed it over. "Here's the equipment list." She watched her mother scan the long list of essential items with a slowly deepening frown.

"It's all right Mum," she said. "Actually, I've got two new jobs."

Both parents looked at her in dismay.

"What do you mean … two jobs?" demanded Mum.

"Doing what?" Dad asked at the very same time.

"We're working for Professor MacBlain," said Tom, watching the frown deepen on his father's face.

"Don't worry," said Beth. "It's not dangerous or anything. Elsie and Connor are doing it too."

"What's not dangerous? And what's that professor got to do with it?" Their mother was slowly coming to the boil.

Tom and Beth exchanged a smile.

Tom shrugged. "Nothing much really," he said. "Just telling jokes to a computer."

Author's Note

Long ago and far way ...

In March 1989, the 215,000 tonne tanker, *Exxon Valdez,* ran aground in Alaska, spilling 11 million gallons of oil into Prince William Sound. It polluted 1,500 miles of coastline, causing the death of about 100,000 seabirds, 16 whales, 147 bald eagles, and thousands of otters and fish. It also destroyed the livelihood of local fishing communities.

You might well think that this has very little to do with you, but the following excerpt from an article written by Nicholas Schoon, published in the *Independent* newspaper in February 1999, may help you to change your mind:

"When the *SeaRiver Mediterranean* sailed up the Firth of Forth last week, she looked much like any other supertanker coming in to take on a huge load of North Sea crude [oil]. But, it emerged last night, the 1000 ft-long ship once sailed under a different name, the most notorious in environmental history — the *Exxon Valdez.*"

Also by Annemarie Allan

Faced with a cold Saturday afternoon stuck at the Institute for Animal Research, Robbie is angry and frustrated at yet another weekend ruined by his father's job. Then a disturbing encounter in the animal house thrusts him into a perilous journey through the stunning but inhospitable landscape of a Highland winter; alone but for two enigmatic travelling companions.

Winner of the Kelpies Prize 2007

*Shortlisted for the Royal Mail Awards
for Scottish Children's Books 2008*